Also by Andy Zach

The Life After Life Chronicles

Reviews of *Zombie Turkeys*, Volume 1 of Life After Life Chronicles

"This book will not only make you laugh out loud, you will be surprised at the tender moments! You'll fly right through it and want more. Mr. Zach has a sense of humor we all need!"- Goodreads

"The yarn is fast-moving from start to finish, opening with the first attack of carnivorous red-eyed wild turkeys very difficult to kill. They can quickly resurrect after death and grow back cut-off limbs. They're led by a tom full of confidence as Zach gives us this tom's perspectives from time to time as he builds his flock into the tens of thousands throughout Illinois and beyond." - Author Dr. Wesley Britton, BookPleasures.com

"Zombie Turkeys is definitely not your typical zombie book. Instead, it is a parody of the standard zombie book, and as such may even be destined for cult status." - Amazon

"I am not one for . . . zombie material, but this was a very entertaining book. The satire kept me reading. Being from Central Illinois I was quite familiar with much of the locations mentioned in the book. I look forward to what is next." - Amazon

"I loved every gobbling, clucking page of this book. It's this hilarious and insane story that wonderfully hits all the right zombie outbreak tropes I love, but done with turkeys and thanksgiving themes. SO FUNNY! I could read about heroic turkey farmers making chipper-shredder last stands for just about forever.!" – Amazon

Reviews of *My Undead Mother-in-law*, Volume 2 of Life After Life Chronicles:

"I am a huge zombie fan, I had thought the genre had worked itself out for a while and then I read this book. I think I have been scarred for life! I foresee months if not years of counseling in my future." – Author Greg Aldridge, Goodreads.com

"Who hasn't had mother in law issues? Well, what if your mother in law was a zombie?

And yet our hero is a zombie avenging evil with her zombie turkeys, bulls, and corgis--all under her command.

Hilarious and heart warming at the same time. The perfect wedding shower gift for the new bride. . . . Can't wait for Andy's next adventure!"

Jacqueline Gillam Fairchild--author Estate of Mind, The Scrap Book Trilogy – Amazon

"This is the kind of mother-in-law we all need--one who can take over a flock of zombie turkeys by tearing the lead turkey into bite-sized pieces. This is just as good as "Zombie Turkeys," folks! Andy Zach is an amazing author! Hope he writes another story soon!" – Amazon

"My Undead Mother-In-Law, while not publicized as a YA story, should appeal to a generation for whom blogging is part of their daily life. Zach even asked a less than famous blogger to write the humorous "Foreword" to the book. That's really what any reader needs to enjoy this strange yarn—a sense of humor and a willingness to lose yourself in a world that never was and never will be. But a world that seems likely to appear once again in yet another sequel." - Author Dr. Wesley Britton, BookPleasures.com

Reviews of *Paranormal Privateers,* Volume 3 of Life After Life Chronicles

Super fun saga following the antics of the Paranormal Privateers. Laugh as they save the world. Who would have thought that the undead would be the saviors of the world? A not-so realistic view of the future of the world. I voluntarily reviewed an ARC of this book. If you like comedy, the paranormal or books about pirates, you will absolutely love Paranormal Privateers. - Amazon

Andy Zach has out done himself. Paranormal Privateers has it all! Follow all your favorite Andy characters as they save the world. Full of action that just zings from one scene to the next, leaving you on the edge of your seat.

And of course the Queen of England is here in all her glory.

I am certain you will love this book.

Who should read it: Any one who has a sense of adventure, all zombie lovers, romance readers who want a new slant, and travel readers who want to take an armchair trip.

Jacqueline Gillam Fairchild--owner, Her Majesty's English Tea Room. Author: Greater Expectations.

Paranormal Privateers is my third go-around with author Andy Zach. As the titles suggest, Zach's world of zombie animals and people aren't meant to terrify readers. Instead, Zach is out to amuse and entertain us with the most unusual situations and scenes most of us will ever experience on the printed page.

This time around, a crew of zombies has a presidential commission and a super-yacht to take on missions the U.S. Military can't. Their leader is the impatient Diane Newby, the "Undead Mother-in-Law" of the previous volume.

A more serious scenario pulls together three storylines as the zombie team infiltrate a North Korean nuclear facility. One of these storylines centers on a North Korean defector who first becomes a zombie, then a Christian, and then he does his best to spread both in a prison camp.

And then . . . we get an alien spaceship bringing powerful aliens to earth. It's almost a completely different book from that point forward, beginning about 2/3 of the way in Paranormal Privateers.

All three volumes of the "Life After Life" series so far are fast-paced romps with minimal character development full of quirky humor and off-the-wall satire. While not billed as YA novels, I see no reason why young adults wouldn't especially enjoy these yarns. There's much about blogging, Skype, and other contemporary matters throughout all the adventures. How about a Kickstarter campaign to fund a cure for the anti-zombie virus? Political correctness? Say "paranormal people," not "zombies."

No reader needs to read the previous books to jump into the action, although it wouldn't hurt to read My Undead Mother-in-Law first to get some character background. But all you need to get into the quirky world of Andy Zach is to have a healthy sense of humor and the willingness to travel to a world that never was and never will be.

This review first appeared at BookPleasures.com on Aug. 6, 2018.

Oops!

Tales of the Zombie Turkey Apocalypse

Andy Zach

Oops! Tales of the Zombie Turkey Apocalypse

Copyright © 2019 - Andy Zach
First Edition, 2019

Author: Andy Zach

Cover Illustration and jacket design: Sean Patrick Flanagan

Formatting – Wild Seas Formatting

Edited by: Dori Harrell
Published by: Jule Inc.
PO Box 10705
Peoria, Illinois 61612
zombieturkeys.com
jms61614-andyzach@yahoo.com
andyzach.net

ISBN: 978-0-9978234-4-8

Published in the United States of America

To my daughters, Tori and Olivia

Acknowledgments

First, credit goes to my children, Tori, Olivia, Ray, and daughter-in-law Jacki. They listened to excerpts and refined my ideas. Tori and Olivia contributed their own short stories to this anthology, with their individual quirkiness.

Then, there's my illustrious illustrator. Sean Flanagan, who created the book art. Both covers and all the story icons reflect his skill.

My editor Dori Harrell edited as I wrote my short stories and helped me publish this collection by Thanksgiving. She gave me encouragement and improved my writing style.

Finally, my wife, Julie. She generates off-the-wall ideas which I work into my stories and then makes the stories better when I read them back to her. Thank you, dear.

Contents

Foreword

Imagine my surprise when Andy Zach asked me to write the foreword to his new book. Here I am, Raven Jones, homemaker, mother of three, and part-time union organizer, writing the foreword for the foremost comic paranormal animal author. His work also covers paranormal and undead humans.

But my story, and that of my husband, Anthony Jones, made it into this anthology, and that's why Andy approached me. At least that's what he said. He's truthful in what he says, but he may have ulterior motives. His brain is often working on something else. I guess that's why he frequently walks into doors.

I was flattered that he wrote Anthony's and my story in with all the other exciting events that have happened before, during, and after the zombie turkey apocalypse. Andy covered that in detail in his documentary, *Zombie Turkeys.* I hear he's negotiating to get it made into a television series.

Andy also wrote my favorite book, *My Undead Mother-In-Law,* and the last of his history series on zombies, *Paranormal Privateers.* The short stories in this collection are the small ripples from the big splashes of these globe-shattering events.

Andy also wrote a non-zombie book about middle-schoolers who became superheroes, *Secret Supers.* He's been a busy author. I got a complimentary copy from him for my kids.

That's enough of an intro. You'll find our story, *Zombie Shift,* inside this collection. Let me know what you think. You can write to me, Raven Jones, through Andy Zach. He protects the anonymity of all his story sources.

Raven Jones
The Zombie Employees Union of Amazin (ZEUofA)
Founder and President

Introduction

Accidents happen. They happen all the time, in real life as well as fiction. If you combine accidents with zombies and genetic engineering, the results get much hairier—and funnier.

I've arranged these stories in time order based upon my Life after Life Chronicles. One of my favorite science fiction authors did that as well: Robert Heinlein with his Past through Tomorrow future history series.

If you want to avoid all possible spoilers, read these stories up until the book cover appears. Then read the book. You can continue without fear afterward.

Many people don't care about spoilers. Read away!

To err is human, to forgive divine.
—Alexander Pope, "An Essay on Criticism, Part II"

The Story of Sound

by Olivia Smith

Once upon a time, there was no sound in the entire world. Everyone could only use signs or gestures to communicate, but they had many problems. Princesses tied to rocks couldn't scream for a hero to rescue them from sea monsters. Sirens couldn't lure sailors with singing. Lightning didn't thunder, and epics went untold.

One queen saw the problem more clearly than anyone else. Her king and prince had both drowned only a short distance from the shore because no one saw them signing for help. The queen sat vigil all night long, and in the morning she sent heralds with large signs in every language to all the humans, elves, dwarves, fairies, leprechauns, and even a dragon. She pled with all to find something that would let creatures communicate without signs or gestures when they couldn't see each other. She promised she would give whatever was in her power to whoever could accomplish this.

Many heroes and heroines went on quests to find a hidden treasure that could do as the queen asked. They found goblins, giants, trolls, and demons, but nothing that allowed them to communicate without sight. Others tried to find a supernatural solution. Witches and wizards cast mighty spells. Shamans made magic sacrifices to gods and goddesses. Sorcerers gestured secret incantations, but they couldn't drum up a magic solution.

Then one oracle had a vision. She managed to scrawl these words before she passed into the afterworld: "Ears are the key to sound." The queen puzzled long and hard over this riddle and finally traveled far to the most powerful sorceress in the town of Noise. The queen showed the sorceress the words of the oracle and asked if she could do anything with them. The sorceress wrote she would try, and she locked herself into her tower for many days. The townspeople could only see the storm clouds gathered around and the lightning bolts that touched the tower.

Finally, the sorceress came back to the queen. In a box she held the creation she had worked so hard to make. She showed the queen two shell-like circles of skin. She fastened them to the side of her head and the queen's head. "These are the answer to your problem," the sorceress said, and the queen heard. "I will show everyone how to make and use them, and then they will all hear sound."

The queen could only gasp her thanks and ask what the sorceress wanted as a reward. The sorceress asked that her town of Noise be given credit for the making of ears and be made famous throughout the land. The queen promised she would do so.

And so the name of Noise was preserved immortal. Everyone now has two ears in memory of the first two made, and everyone can hear sound. However, sometimes sound can become too much. Then people can only curse that Noise.

Olivia Smith is a new author, appearing for the first time in Oops! *I wondered if her fairy-tale style story would fit, but decided its accidental, serendipitous style fit the theme of my anthology well. Olivia, in addition to writing, also works as an electrical engineer.*

A Phoenix Tale

by Andy Zach

I left the air-conditioned comfort of the taxi, and the sights, sounds, and smells of the old bazaar in Jeddah assailed me: a robe-clad man on camel plodded by, an adjacent fishmonger added his smell to the fresh dung in the street, and the hawkers yelled their wares.

I could only speak Arabic at a middle school level, but as I strolled through the bazaar, I heard "Fresh dates!"..."Highest quality rugs!"..."Finest gold jewelry!"... "Ancient books! The rarest in Saudi Arabia!"

My head snapped around. A bald, stumpy man in a white caftan saw me look and said, "Books? You want ancient books?"

"Yes." I spoke carefully, knowing my poor accent. "Can you speak English?" I didn't have much hope.

"Of course, my friend. Come into my shop."

It was just a nook in the wall but shielded by an awning, with four bookshelves covered in old books. In the back was a worn rug, and as he sat cross-legged, he gestured for me to sit on some cushions. I did, enjoying the classic ambiance of Arab hospitality. What a contrast from the hubbub of the US and the UK in the '80s!

"Muhammed al-Jeddah at your service." His English was excellent.

"Andy Zach, doctoral student and seeker of Arabic manuscripts on the phoenix."

"Ah. Let us enjoy some refreshments before we get to business."

"Thank you so much for your hospitality. I am weary with jet lag. I just arrived yesterday."

He murmured through a curtain in the back. A woman in a hajib came forward with a small silver coffeepot. She glanced at me. I saw almond eyes of darkest brown, shining with curiosity. A whiff of strong coffee from the pot and the scent of jasmine from the girl greeted my nose.

"My daughter, Myriam. She is my life since the death of my wife."

"My condolences on your loss. I understand one never gets over the death of a loved one."

"So true. Yet in my daughter, I see my wife as when I first married her twenty years ago. Allah has been good to me, leaving me a living memory."

I nodded and sipped my coffee. Magnificently hot, strong enough for coffee liquor, and sweet as an entire candy shop, the flavors and heat warred in my mouth.

Muhammed sipped his cup, sighed contentedly, and said, "There is nothing like fine coffee."

"It's quite remarkable. I've never had anything like it."

He smiled. "I'm glad you like it. Here. Enjoy these fresh dates and figs."

I bit a juicy fig and had to wipe my mouth. "Amazing! It's like I've never had a fig before!"

"Yes. Our tree produces the finest figs in Saudi Arabia."

"You are blessed indeed, Muhammed."

He sighed with a smile and looked off in the distance.

Trying to broach the subject of phoenix manuscripts tactfully, I said, "I have been studying phoenixes for many months already."

"You must be a diligent scholar to come all the way from America."

"I *do* have a one-track mind," I admitted. "I'm enrolled at Cambridge, College of Paranormal Animals, so I didn't come as far as that."

"I've never heard of the College of Paranormal Animals."

"I'm not surprised. My advisor, Dr. Edwina McDougal, created it to suit my doctoral interest."

"Did you see the copy of *Solomon and the Phoenix* in the British Library from the wondrous library of Tipu Sultan, ruler of Mysore?"

Impressed by his knowledge, I said, "Yes, that was one the manuscripts I studied. In fact, that's why I'm here. I'm looking for another such manuscript to shed light on the phoenix. The historian Herodotus said the phoenix originated in Arabia."

"Ah yes," he said, as if just remembering my original request. "Have you read the *Kitab al-Bulhan?*"

Kitab al-Bulhan, which translated to *Book of Wonders*, was a fourteenth-century Arabic source on the phoenix. It included a discourse on the simurgh, or phoenix. "Yes indeed. It's well named."

"I do not have a copy of *Kitab al-Bulhan*," he said with a sigh. "I do have a few pages that resemble it."

"Oh? May I see them?" I tried to keep my excitement out of my voice, but failed. So much for my negotiating skills. I had intended to negotiate fiercely for anything.

"I'm sorry, but they appear to be torn out of a book. That is why it was not worthy to be shown in my shop. You surely would not want to see such inferior merchandise, would you?"

Muhammed was in full negotiating mode. Disparage your merchandise to see how much the client wants it. "Ordinarily no, but my curiosity must be satisfied."

Without a word he got up and ducked through the curtain. He came back with a few dusty pages of parchment. The dust did not hide the brilliantly colored phoenix adorning one page.

I gasped. "This matches the *Book of Wonder* I saw in the British Museum!"

"Yet I fear it is not the same. For I too have seen that, and these pages do not match."

Although I was poor at listening to and speaking Arabic, my hours of study enabled me to read the two accompanying pages. They were different from the standard *Book of Wonder*. The writer spoke of studying the phoenix in Western Arabia. He said it nested in the hills above the Pishon river. I knew from my studies on the Garden of Eden that the biblical river Pishon had dried up in the millennia since and now corresponded to the Wadi al-Batin. 'That was quite close to Jeddah, less than a hundred miles away!

"Oh my! This is a dream come true!" All thoughts of negotiating evaporated as I saw my goal within reach. Imagine if I could get a blood sample of the phoenix! I might be able to isolate its regeneration gene! All my undergraduate biological studies would bear fruit! I would achieve my PhD in animal revivification at the Cambridge College of Paranormal Animals!

Rereading the pages carefully, I noted the anonymous author said the nest was two or three days' journey from the origin of the Pishon, near Medina. That'd be sixty miles by foot or ninety to a hundred and twenty by camel or horse.

"This seems to be a copy of *Katib al-Bulhan* with additional notes."

"Perhaps. The illustration is definitely a copy. I believe the notes are a copy of a yet older manuscript."

"Oh? Why do you say that?"

"The Arabic style is very old, pre-Mohammed, may his name be praised." He paused. "Is this something you want for yourself?" asked Muhammed.

"I'd love to own it, but I doubt I have the money to buy something so valuable. You'd be better off selling it to a museum or holding an auction."

"Money! I have enough. I delight in seeing someone who appreciates the beauty of this manuscript. What can you afford?"

"I can't really say. You see, I have to go on an expedition looking for the phoenix mentioned here. That was my purpose for coming to your land. After that, I don't know how much money I'll have left."

"To the Pishon river? Isn't that the Wadi al-Batin today?"

Once again Muhammed impressed me. I'd thought that was a rather obscure fact. "Yes, you're correct."

"How far must you travel along the wadi?"

"Probably a hundred and fifty miles from Medina, to be sure."

"I believe my cousin's husband can help. He takes people on tours. May I call him to check?"

"Of course."

Muhammed called through the curtain to Myriam. She brought an antique French phone on a long cord. He dialed and talked rapidly on it. After he hung up, he said, "Good news! My cousin Hassan will gladly take you to search for the simurgh."

"That's wonderful! But will I be able to afford him?"

"Do not worry about money. If you find the phoenix, that will be payment enough for me." He smiled.

Of course. If I found the phoenix using his manuscript, that would multiply the value of his document!

"When can we leave?"

"Tomorrow evening would be best. In the desert, you should travel by night. I assume you are prepared for desert travel?"

"Yes, my clothing covers both the cool nights and the hot days."

"Good."

The following evening I met Hassan and Muhammed in the souk by the bookshop. They led me to a battered Land Rover. I could barely see the dark-green paint through the scrapes, sand, and mud.

I had checked out of the hotel and held my only bag. I had my detailed map of Saudi Arabia with me, a canteen of water, pemmican, beef jerky, and dried fruit for several days.

"My cousin al-Hassan." Muhammed introduced us.

"Salam Alaikum," the cousin said formally, with his hands together.

"Wa-Alaikum-Salaam." I replied properly to his greeting of peace with, "And peace to you. I am Andy Zach."

"Welcome to my adventure tour. Muhammed has told me of your plan to explore Wadi al-Batin's source."

"Indeed yes. I have it charted on my map"—I gestured to it—"but I have no idea of the best way to get there."

"There is no best way in the desert. There is only the way you find."

That didn't give me much confidence. But what choice did I have? I had to find out if a phoenix was a mere mythological creature or an actual source of revivification for animals. I showed Hassan my map of the ancient Pishon river and the various wadis composing it.

"Wadi al-Batin is at the mouth of the Pishon, indicated by the ancient alluvial fan. Then there is Wadi Rimah, which leads to Wadi al-Batin. Proceeding upstream, that wadi splits into Wadi Qahd on the northwest and the Wadi al Jarir on the southwest. Which one should we investigate the source of the Pishon? Wadi al Jarir goes further uphill to the Mahd adh Dhahab gold mine, exactly as the Bible says: 'The River Pishon encompasses the whole land of Havilah, where there is gold.' So can you get us to the beginning of Wadi al Jarir?" I concluded.

"Yes. We'll go along the coast and then take the old mining road. Once we're there, we'll go to the Wadi al Jarir." He smiled. "Then you'll have to take over, young man."

I nodded more assuredly than I felt. Could I find the source of a river that hadn't flowed for over thirty-five hundred years? Could I find the nest of a bird that hadn't been seen in over two thousand?

Meanwhile, Hassan introduced me to his aide, Omar.

A skinny youth with curly hair grinned at me, showing crooked teeth. "I only speak Arabic," he said.

"I speak a little," I replied as we shook hands. I towered over him.

"Good! We'll get along fine!"

"Omar will help with the driving," Hassan said. "I'm no good driving at night. Too old. But not as old as my cousin!" He looked at Muhammed.

"True, true. We can't all be as young as you are, Hassan or Omar." Muhammed stared at Omar with a frown, as if something was wrong. "What happened to your regular driver, Abdullah?"

"Ah, he fell sick. He recommended his friend Omar."

"Inshallah," Muhammed said, like a prayer.

"Inshallah," agreed Hassan and Omar. "God's will be done" was a rough translation.

I wasn't Islamic, but I said, "Amen!"

We left by ten and traveled through the dark night. First, we followed the Red Sea north, and then we took the road into the mountain highlands to Mahd adh Dhahab. Hassan soon fell asleep in the backseat, but Omar chattered in Arabic the whole way as I sat next to him.

"So what do you seek in Mahd adh Dhahab?"

"The origin of the old river Pishon." I didn't know the word for "ancient" in Arabic.

"Ah! I have heard of that river! It began in the mountains and flowed to the gulf many years ago."

Surprised, I asked, "How did you hear?"

"I read—a lot." Here he lapsed into English and gave me his big grin.

"How much English do you speak?"

"Just a little. But I understand a lot!"

So we continued, me in my broken Arabic and he in his occasional English phrase. The five hours went quickly, and when we reached Mahd adh Dhahab, Omar drove to the outskirts and pulled off the road. Hassan awoke.

"Here we are. We're in the Wadi al Jarir. Now where do we

go, Mr. Zach?"

I slid out of the Rover and stretched my legs. In the moonlight, I could see the mountains to the north of the wadi. "How far can we get into the mountains from here?"

"As far as you dare," Hassan said with equanimity.

I laughed. "You'll find I dare a great deal. How much danger is there driving off road in the dark?" It felt good to be talking in English again.

"Only from hidden rocks and ruts. We'll avoid them, inshallah."

"Let us go then!"

We followed the bottom of the wadi up to the foothills. I picked a valley leading up to the highest point. The jostling got much worse. Several times I thought we broke something, but Hassan said, "No problem! Do not worry!"

We had just climbed a steep slope and had been headed slightly downhill, before another, steeper slope.

Crash! The front left wheel slid into a hole, and I felt the bottom of the car bottom out.

"No problem!" In Arabic, Hassam said to Omar, "Back us up."

The wheels spun uselessly.

"No problem! Omar, you push. I'll drive."

"Let me help." I hopped out of the Rover.

It felt odd to be paired with a five-foot Arab boy who probably didn't weigh more than a hundred pounds, half my weight. We pushed and pulled gamely as Hassan rocked the car forward and back. The front wheel wouldn't edge out of the hole. I couldn't see how deep it was in the dark, but the wheel seemed to be hanging in the air.

The Land Rover teetered on the rocky berm, and neither the front nor rear wheels achieved good traction.

"We need a lever to pry us out of the hole," I said.

"Dawn is coming," Hassan said, pointing to the lightening eastern horizon. "That will help. Let us make coffee and drink it until then."

"Good idea."

We sipped our small cups of strong, sweet coffee made from the electric coffeepot Hassan plugged into the cigarette lighter as we sat watching the sunrise. We discussed where we could get a lever. No trees were in sight. It was six miles back to Mahd adh Dhahab, which we could see in the distance.

"Hassan, you seem very calm, with your car stranded here."

"Inshallah. We'll go back to Mahd adh Dhahab, or we'll find a way out."

"Hey, look at this!" Omar called. He had been examining the hole in which we were stuck, trying to find the bottom. We ran around to the front wheel, and next to it was Omar's head. He had wriggled his body into the hole and was standing upright.

"I hope the car doesn't fall!" I switched to Arabic again to match him.

"Ha! Inshallah! The hole is much deeper than I am. Watch!" His head disappeared, and then he called from underground, "It gets bigger! It's a cave! Get a light!"

I shone my flashlight down. I could see perhaps ten feet down, but no Omar, only rocks.

"Hand me the light!" He popped back up from under the wheel.

I handed it to him.

I really wanted to follow him, but there was no way I could fit. Unless... "Hassan! If I take off the wheel, I could go down there too!"

He peered at the hole and the wheel. "I am curious too. Let's do it."

With the wheel off, both Hassan and I wriggled past the axle and down the hole. It descended at a forty-five-degree angle for fifteen feet and leveled out. It was almost high enough for me to stand.

"Look!" Omar cried. "Water!"

Far in the back of the cave was a small pool in a depression in the rock. I studied the walls of the cave. Everything was smooth and weathered, but there were no stalactites or stalagmites, as I would expect to see in caves in the United States.

"I wonder if this is the Pishon source? Everything is eroded like the bottom of a river."

"Perhaps so," Hassan agreed with caution.

Looking upward from the water pool, I saw a high, domed ceiling. The water erosion continued upward for ten feet, and then the rocks were jagged and rough.

"We've gotten this far. I might as well explore a little further." With a leap, I grabbed a ledge about nine feet above and pulled myself up. I enjoyed rock climbing, and this was easy compared to some cliffs I had scaled.

From the ledge, I surveyed the upper portion of the dome. Opposite me, twenty-five feet away, was a dark opening. I shone the flashlight on it but couldn't see much. Studying the adjacent rock walls, I plotted a path to the recess.

Clipping my flashlight to my belt, I traversed along the vertical walls to the recess. With a final jump, I plopped onto the lip that hid the recess from below. In the recess, I found a circle of stones four feet in diameter. The stones were all weathered smooth and round like the river stones below. How had they gotten up here? And who had placed them? And when?

"What is it? What do you see?" Omar cried in Arabic.

"A circle. Someone has placed stones here in a circle."

"Oho! Maybe it's the simurgh!"

The phoenix? I hadn't thought of that. But this could have been the source of the Pishon, and the circle of stones was like a nest. I stirred the dirt in the middle of the stones. It was darker than the rest of the dust, but it was just dirt.

"Here. Take my camera. You must take pictures." Hassan held up the camera.

"Let me help!" Omar grabbed the camera and then, like a monkey, climbed the wall to the ledge.

"My! You'd do well in rock climbing!"

"I love to climb." He handed me the camera, complete with flashbulbs. I took as many pictures as I had flashbulbs, eight.

"Take one of the stones as well," Hassan called from below.

I selected the largest and smoothest. It didn't weigh as much as I'd expected. I studied the light-gray surface carefully. It was smooth, with tiny pockmarks. It didn't weigh as much as stone, but perhaps as much as a dense wood. I checked the other stones. They were all heavier but smaller and just like worn river rocks. They were also a darker gray.

"Hassan, can you catch this? It weighs maybe five pounds."

He caught it.

We climbed our way back to the surface after refilling our canteens. The sun was just over the horizon.

"If we're going to Mahd adh Dhahab, we'd better go before it gets hotter," I commented.

"It'll take two hours there and two hours back," Hassan said. "Be prepared for heat and sun. Drink all your water there, refill your canteen, and drink it all on the way back. You can't have too much water in the desert."

"That makes sense. I think if I jog, I can make it in half the time." I actually thought I could make it in less than an hour, but I wasn't sure about the terrain.

"Be very careful. If you break a leg, you could die."

"I know."

"Go to the service station in town and see if they have a big pry bar."

"I will go too," Omar said in English.

"What?" said Hassan and I simultaneously, me in English, Hassan in Arabic.

"I like to run. And I can translate," Omar said in Arabic.

"You said you didn't speak English."

"I don't speak it very much. But I understand it enough to understand you."

"OK, let's go."

The terrain was rough. I could only run half the time. Omar had no trouble keeping up with my long legs. He ran lightly, like a bird or a fawn. We made it there in an hour.

The service station had a six-foot pry bar. They gladly let us borrow it. They were willing to drive us to our car in their truck. We all crammed in the cab, and the ancient four-wheeler climbed up the slope. The driver, Nasri, began grumbling about the rough terrain soon after we left the road, and when he saw the final climb to our Land Rover, he refused to go farther.

"You can carry it from here," he said.

And we did. He had still saved us half an hour.

Hassan was not visible in the blazing sun. Unsurprisingly, he had gone into the cool cave. The surprise was the thread of smoke coming from the cave entrance.

Why would Hassan build a fire? I wondered.

I went below, with Oman following me through the smoky air.

At the bottom, Hassan sat with a wet cloth across his face and a small kerosene stove he had carried down. The big stone was on the burner, heating up.

"What are you doing?"

"I'm curious like you are. This stone is not stone at all. Yet it's not wood either. I've been heating this for an hour, and it hasn't charred at all."

"Perhaps it's volcanic. Those rocks are porous. Do you have a hammer?"

"Back in the car."

I was willing to try and crack this rock. I climbed back out and retrieved the hammer. Just as I was about to descend, I heard an audible *crack*, and Hassan and Omar both yelled.

"Are you OK?" I called into the hole. Then rushing past my head came a brilliant red, yellow, and blue bird. A phoenix!

"AH!" I yelled as it zoomed by me.

"Ka-eee!" it called, climbing rapidly, circling around, and then heading east and out of sight.

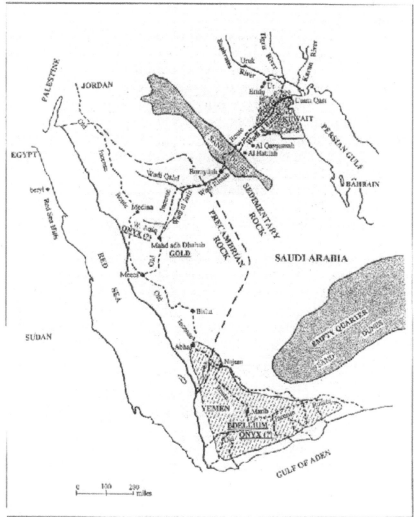

Fig. 1. Map of the "land of Havilah" (Saudi Arabia and Yemen) showing the location of the old incense routes (short dashes); the area where bdellium was grown (diagonal hatching); Precambrian and sedimentary rock (long dashes between the two areas); the gravel fan deposited by the Pishon River (gravel symbol) and other places mentioned in the text.

I sat down gasping, staring at the eastern horizon, where it had disappeared. So. The manuscript was true. The phoenix did nest at the source of the Pishon, now dried. Why hadn't the egg hatched, possibly for thousands of years?

Normally the phoenix builds its nest, sets the nest and itself on fire, and out of the ashes comes the egg, which hatches. Obviously, the egg needs heat to hatch, which Hassan thoughtfully supplied through his kerosene stove. If it didn't hatch, then the blaze didn't create enough heat or didn't last long enough.

Regardless, the phoenix disappeared from history, except for the lingering records in Greece, Egypt, the Middle East, and Asia. To have come so close to capturing the fabled bird and have it fly away! Where would it have gone?

According to legend, the phoenix flew from Arabia to Egypt after it hatched. That must be why it flew east. But...it also carried the ashes of its nest and deposited them in a temple by the Nile. The eagle-sized bird I saw carried nothing. Perhaps it would come back?

While I ruminated on the dusty hillside, Hassan and Omar climbed from the cave.

"Was that...the simurgh?" Hassan gasped.

"Yes."

"It burst from the egg with a blaze of flame. I could feel its heat as it flew by me. Where did it go?"

"To the east. I think it'll come back."

"Why do you say so?"

"I believe it needs to gather the ashes of its nest. That seems to be instinctual."

"What will you do next, Andy?"

"Try to capture it."

"The simurgh is a large and powerful bird."

"I brought sedative doses suitable for shooting from my tranquilizer pistol."

"Will you shoot it as it enters the cave?"

"No, I'll wait inside the cave, hidden, while it seeks its nest. Could you take pictures, Hassan?"

"Yes."

"Could I help?" Omar asked.

"Yes. Let's get the car repaired and get some date palm branches."

"Why?"

"One of the traditions about the phoenix is that it builds its nest from the branches of the date palm. Thus, it would look for ashes of the date palm by its nest. Let's burn some and give it the ashes it needs."

Together, Omar and I levered the car out of the hole. Hassan and I left Omar with the tranquilizer pistol while we drove to the nearest oasis, back in the city. Returning with the palm branches, we built a fire of them, then gathered the ashes and carried them into the midst of the stone circle where we'd found the phoenix egg.

The setting sun provided only lurid light into the cave. I huddled in an alcove above and across from the phoenix's nest with my pistol. Hassan hid with his camera beneath a dark tarp on the floor.

My legs cramped, and I shifted back and forth to stretch my muscles. I'd been waiting for hours now. I'd give up after sunset.

Whoosh! Click. A flash of red, yellow, and blue landed in the nest. It carried a ball of something. I caught a scent. Myrrh! Myrrh resin was what the phoenix used to gather its ashes for the trip to Egypt.

I aimed carefully for the phoenix's breast. I was a capable shot, having been in the NRA since my Boy Scout years. The last thing I wanted was to harm the bird after it had survived thousands of years. I figured a shot in the breast was least likely to cause injury.

Crack! The gun sounded louder in the enclosed dome. The phoenix exploded into action! It leapt into the air and flew away even faster than it had come.

I was sure I'd hit it. It should collapse soon. I scrambled down and raced past Hassan and out of the cave.

Omar was there holding the other camera, his eyes wide with amazement.

"What happened when the phoenix came out?" I asked.

"Lightning. It flew like lightning," he said in Arabic.

"Flew where? You get pictures?" I spoke more quickly than I ever had in Arabic.

"There." He pointed to the purpling eastern horizon. "I have two pictures."

"And..." He stooped to the ground. "This fell from the phoenix."

It was the tranquilizing dart. I studied it. It was empty; the bird had gotten the full dose. It shouldn't have been able to fly more than a dozen feet. But it had flown out of sight to the east.

I shouldn't have expected normal drugs to work on paranormal birds.

"Have we lost the simurgh?" Hassan asked quietly.

"For now. My tranquilizer didn't work."

"Will simurgh return?"

"Let's see if it took the myrrh egg."

I climbed back into the cave and up to the phoenix's nest and saw the discarded egg. The phoenix had hollowed it out and filled it half full of ashes.

"The phoenix will probably come back!" I called down to Hassan and Omar. "It'll want its egg and ashes."

Later, as we ate around the kerosene stove, I asked my companions, "Normal drugs didn't work on the phoenix. What can I use?"

"The phoenix can heal itself. It would have to be something very powerful."

Omar laughed. "I have some hashish!"

I laughed too. "Why do you have that?"

He shrugged. "For injuries. It is good for pain."

"True. I'm willing to try anything. Perhaps even a poison."

"I saw some wormwood on the way to town."

"Really? That's what they use for absinthe. That's very powerful. Any other ideas? I think we'll only get one more chance at this bird. I can't believe how fast it flies!"

Hassan barked a laugh. "I have a quart of 'sid' in the car." Keeping a straight face, he said, "It's for disinfecting wounds."

I laughed too. "Sid" or "siddiq" was Arabic for "my friend." Siddiq was home-brewed alcohol, like moonshine in the States—and just as illegal in Saudi Arabia, a supposedly "dry" country.

"Cut or uncut?" I asked. Normally siddiq is diluted two to one prior to drinking with a mixer.

"Uncut."

"Whew! That makes it one-hundred-fifty- to one-hundred-eighty-proof alcohol. Kissing cousin to paint stripper." I thought a moment."OK, let's do this. I'll take the hashish and let it soak in the sid overnight. Then we'll collect the wormwood tomorrow, grind it up, and add that to the mixture. Then I'll put it into the trank capsule and give it a try on the phoenix. If this doesn't work, I'll have to try a net."

"Supposedly the simurgh is impossible to catch," Hassan said with audible doubt.

"Yes. It's Hobson's choice. When you have one alternative, you try it. I doubt anyone in all history has tried this concoction. It'd definitely be poisonous to a human. For a paranormal bird with supernatural recuperative powers, who knows what'll happen?"

Hassan and Omar contributed their drugs, and I blended them in Hassan's mason jar labeled in Arabic: *Disinfectant: do not drink.*

I got dizzy just from breathing the fumes. I was pretty sure the opioids in hashish were soluble in alcohol, as was absinthe. I sealed the jar tightly.

"I won't have any trouble sleeping tonight."

"When should we go for the wormwood? What if the phoenix comes with the dawn tomorrow?" Omar asked.

"I hadn't thought of that," I admitted. "It makes sense too. The phoenix is highly intelligent, and it may try to slip into the cave the first thing tomorrow morning, even before dawn." There! I'd said a whole sentence in Arabic without translating it first.

"Can we get it tonight?" Omar asked.

"In the dark?" Aside from the small town, there was no light in the desert.

"There'll be a little moon, and I know exactly where it is. We walked right by the bush."

"It's worth a try."

"You boys enjoy your search in the dark. I'll sit here and drink tea and read," Hassan said, turning a page in his book.

I recognized it—an old Arabic edition of *The Tales of Sinbad*, a late addition to *One Thousand and One Nights*

Driving carefully, I retraced our path from this morning. Even driving slowly, we went twice as fast as we could walk.

"Slow! Here it is, to the left," Omar said suddenly.

I could see nothing, but he stepped out confidently. I followed.

"Here." In a gully I saw a small bush perhaps three feet high. Examining the leaves with my flashlight, I saw they were gray green on top, white below.

"How much do you think we need, Omar?"

He shrugged. "My mother only used a few branches to make medicine."

I took a bundle of fresh and a bundle of old branches. I didn't know which would have the essence more strongly.

We made it back, where we discovered Hassan sound

asleep. I also saw the jar of sid and hashish had leaked! It tipped on its side, and only about half the liquid was still there.

"Crap!"

"Perhaps this is good," Omar said.

"How?"

"Perhaps it will make the hashish more concentrated."

"Hmmm. Good idea. Let me try something." I mashed the wormwood branches and leaves into a paste and then put them in the jar. I took a cooking pot and poured water from my canteen into it. Then I placed the pot on the cookstove. Once it was boiling, I put the sid-hashish-wormwood mixture into the boiling water. I knew alcohol boiled at a lower temperature than water. Soon it was boiling vigorously.

I watched the mixture carefully, and when it was less than a cup, I took it out.

"I'll let this steep overnight. Let's get some sleep. We'll have to get up well before light." I set my small, leather-covered traveler alarm clock and left the world of waking like a falling plinth.

I dreamed of a fire-alarm drill in my high school. Everyone was yelling, "Get out! Get out!"

"Get up!" Omar yelled, shaking me.

"Ah!" I rubbed my sleep-filled eyes and saw the eastern horizon was slightly light, while the stars blazed above in the indigo desert sky. Hassan snored, oblivious to all.

As I filled a tranquilizer dart with the hashish and absinthe tincture, I said, "I'd better use the tarp for cover. I don't want the phoenix to see me and fly away."

"I will hide by the pool and take pictures," Omar said.

We quickly moved into position. Less than an hour later, *whoosh*, and a dazzling yellow-and-scarlet bird lighted in the nest. It had two long blue feathers in its tail. It quickly packed the egg with ashes and then began to seal the myrrh ball with its beak and clawed foot. I shot it from under the tarp.

It screamed "Kee-ah!" and flew away, as Omar had said, like lightning. I blinked, trying to process what I had seen. One instant it had been there with the dart sticking out of its scarlet breast. Then with a flicker of movement, it and the egg vanished up the tunnel. The only comparable acceleration I had ever seen was a hummingbird zipping out of sight from a standstill at a feeder in an eye blink. The dart fell off during that sudden movement and clicked on the stone below.

I sighed. We'd lost it for good. It had simply ignored the dart's effect. It had no reason to return for five hundred years. According to the phoenix legend, it builds a pyre every five hundred years, burns itself, and leaves an egg behind. The egg then hatches. In this cave, it looked like the egg hadn't hatched after the fire. Perhaps a flood had quenched the fire?

"I got some good pictures," Omar said. "Did you shoot it?"

"Yes. It didn't seem to do any good."

"Inshallah. Perhaps it is for the best."

Coming out of the cave, Hassan greeted us. "Good news, Mr. Zach! I got some good pictures of the phoenix as it left the cave."

"I'm surprised. It moved faster than my eye could track."

"Perhaps it was slowed by the drug. It moved no faster than a normal eagle or heron. It vanished over that ridge to the east."

"Was it climbing?"

"No, it was level."

"Hmmm. I've come this far. Let me see if it came down in the wadi over the ridge."

"I will stay behind and prepare tea," Hassan said.

"I will come with you," Omar said.

"Thank you, both."

To the top of the hill I trudged, carrying my binoculars.

"Do you think the phoenix will be there?" Omar said.

"I hope so, but I also don't want to hope too much."

"I think it will. I think the hashish got to it. What will you do when you get it?"

"I plan to take a blood sample and let it go. If it's there."

"I'm sure you'll get it. Inshallah."

We got to the top and looked into the next wadi. Dry, gray stone greeted us. I scanned up the wadi to the peak of the mountain and down to the base. No sign of the phoenix.

"Should we climb the next ridge too?" Omar asked.

"Let's do it."

Down into the wadi we clambered. Back up the next, steeper ridge, crawling on our hands and knees in the sliding scree. I paused to tug my leather gloves on to protect my palms from the sharp rocks.

At the top, the dazzling rising sun greeted us. There was

no wadi, just a broad, sloping shoulder of the mountain. Looking down the slope, I saw nothing. Looking up, I saw nothing.

"What's that?" Omar asked, pointing toward the top of the mountain.

"What's what?" I said in English, too tired and discouraged to translate in my head. I looked where he pointed but saw nothing.

"I see something!" He ran up the slope like a goat.

I followed him clumsily, feeling like a draft horse chasing a thoroughbred Arabian.

Near the peak, Omar knelt by a bush of myrrh. I saw it had its top branches broken off. That must have been what he saw. In a dark, sharp shadow, in a gully at the base, lay the phoenix.

"Is it alive?" I panted.

"Yes, but soundly asleep."

Even in repose, in the shade, the plumage dazzled. Iridescent scarlet, metallic gold, and shimmery blue feathers clothed a bird nobler than an eagle. I took an empty tranquilizer dart and stuck the bird in the breast. I had an eyedropper from my medicine kit, which I used to coax drops of that precious blood from the world's only phoenix into my capsule, through the hollow dart.

It took over ten minutes to fill it. I noticed the phoenix was exceedingly hot blooded—enough that the blood's heat hurt my fingers through the capsule. I wrapped my shirt around it to protect them.

"There. I'm done. Let's take it back to the cave and place it and its egg in its nest."

As we climbed down, we took turns carrying the phoenix in our arms. It was too hot to hold for long.

"Omar, you'd better take it now. It's burning me."

He wrapped it in the bottom of his robe. Then turning his midnight-brown eyes to me, he said in perfect English, "I haven't been honest with you."

"Ah. I see. Why did you hide your beautiful English?"

"To disguise me from Hassan."

"Why would you do that?"

"If he knew who I was, he'd return me home, and I wouldn't get to go on this adventure."

"So who are you?"

"Do you promise not to tell?"

"Have you committed a crime?"

He laughed. "No, except in running from my father."

"It's good for a teenaged boy to have adventures. I won't tell your secret."

"How about a teenaged girl?"

"Them too. What are you saying?" A suspicion arose in my thoughts.

"I am a girl," he—no—she said simply.

"Oh! I see the issue."

"You only see part of it. My father is Muhammed al-Jeddah. I am Myriam."

Rocked by this revelation, I stared frankly at her. Was this dirty little urchin the dark-eyed girl smelling of jasmine? "Won't he worry about you?"

"Extremely. He worries all the time as it is. He needs to see I am growing and need freedom and that he can trust me."

"He may try to marry you off."

"I hope so. I have someone in mind."

"Doesn't he select your husband?"

"Theoretically, yes. Practically, he'll be so relieved to have me back, I believe he'll go along with my idea."

"I hope he does, for your sake. I've grown to like you, Omar or Myriam, dirty or clean."

She laughed and skipped away down the slope to our camp, while I trudged on, carrying the hot and heavy phoenix.

We placed the phoenix and its egg carefully in its nest in the cave. We packed our Land Rover and headed home with our precious cargo. I stopped in Mahd adh Dhahab and bought a cooler and dry ice and packed the blood capsule.

"Omar" slipped away as soon as we returned to Jeddah. "I must go and see how Abdullah is feeling." I smiled at him/her.

After checking back into my hotel and cleaning up, I went to Muhammed's stall in the bazaar. It was closed. I knocked on the door to his home at the back of the stall.

"Who is it?" came a weary voice.

"Andy Zach."

"I'm sorry, Andy. I cannot see you today. I am in grief over my daughter, Myriam. She has disappeared, and I cannot find her."

"I have good news for you, my friend! I saw her when I returned to Jeddah. She should be home soon!" There. That skirted the truth very nicely.

Muhammed's tear-stained face brightened. "Are you sure?"

"Absolutely! I last saw her near my hotel, and she waved at me!" Again, true.

"Oh, now you must come in. I must prepare for her!"

"Allow me to help you, my friend. And I have more good news."

"I cannot be any happier than to see my daughter again. I can't imagine what happened to her. She disappeared the day you and Hassan left."

"I'm sure she'll have an interesting story. The other good news is, we captured the phoenix, the simurgh!"

"Wonder upon wonder! Still, it pales to nothing compared to my daughter coming home. But tell me anyway."

As we cleaned the house, I told him the tale of the phoenix, its nest, its egg hatching, and its escape. I told him of it shrugging off the tranquilizer and then succumbing to the hashish, absinthe, and siddiq mixture.

"Siddiq! Of the three drugs, that is the most potent!" He smiled. "Not that I've ever tasted it."

"Perhaps you used some for disinfecting a wound?"

"The very thing! How prescient you are! Yes, I cleaned my wound and grew dizzy from the fumes. How wise is Mohammed to forbid it!"

"Inshallah," I said piously.

After he bathed, Muhammed dressed in his finest white thob, or robe, with his red-and-white keffiyeh.

"Now I will open my shop in my finest garb so I may watch for my daughter."

I helped him roll the bookshelves from the storage closet and set up the canopy. He beamed and called at passersby in the bazaar and soon attracted considerable business. Even when he was seated at coffee with customers, his eyes roamed the crowded alley outside the store.

Muhammed had just made a big sale when his neck jerked around. Following his gaze, I saw a woman in a black hajib approaching.

"Myriam!" he yelled. Heedless of his dignity and formal

wear, he ran to her.

They embraced, and he lifted her off her feet and then practically carried her to his shop.

"I will close for the rest of the day. I must celebrate my daughter's return!"

I closed up the shop, and then Muhammed called from the door, "Andy! You must celebrate with me! You brought me the news and my daughter!"

I came into their home. The caterers had arrived, and they had laid out a feast of goat, lamb, rice, dates, ripe figs from Muhammed's own tree, and freshly baked pita bread.

"Sit! Sit!" Muhammed insisted. "My joy overflows, and I must spill it on you. I will serve you and my daughter today. For too many years she has served me, an old man, with no thanks."

Myriam removed her hajib, showing her sparkling eyes. "Father, thank you. I have a great story to tell you."

"Please, let it wait. First, let us feast and rejoice!"

A group of musicians began playing softly.

After the feast, Muhammed turned to me and said, "First, let Andy tell the tale of the phoenix. Leave out no detail, for Myriam has not heard it, and I know you only gave me a cursory account."

I spent the next hour recounting the whole story, interrupted by questions from both Muhammed and Myriam. She usually queried about Omar, asking me for my opinion and view of him, and usually with a sly smile.

Muhammed commented, "I had not met this Omar before and was doubtful of him. But from your account, he seems to be a fine young man."

"I am so jealous of him, to be able to go on such an adventure!" Myriam complained.

"You have been on your own adventure. It is time for you to tell of it."

"Thank you, Father. I am eager to speak of it. But I must have your promise that you will not punish me for running away without telling you."

"Myriam, I am hurt that you would think I would punish you when I am full of joy at your return. If I intended to punish you, would I throw a feast?"

"No."

"Would I run in the marketplace in my best clothing to carry you to our home?"

"No."

"There is your promise."

"Very well. I will tell you my story. It began the night you and Andy contacted Hassan to take Andy to the source of the Pishon. My heart burned within me to go on that adventure with the young American student. But I knew you would never permit it, Father.

"That night, after you went to bed, I cut my hair like a boy. I dressed in the clothing of a serving boy. I had a dental prosthetic I had previously made for just this type of occasion, to give me crooked teeth. I smudged my face with dirt. And I got Abdullah to let me go in his place."

Myriam then related the whole of the phoenix story from her point of view. She concluded, "I left Andy at his hotel, went back to Abdullah, got my clothing, washed up, and walked home. I have never been so happy in my life, since mother died, to be on this adventure. Now what do you say, Father?"

Muhammed's face had been blank since Myriam began her story. He looked somberly at her, and slowly a tear trickled from his eye.

"My heart is at war with itself. I am proud of your character and accomplishments, and ashamed. Not ashamed of you, but of me. I should have found a husband for you this year. You are now the age your mother was when she married me."

"Have you considered Abdullah?"

"Have you?" Muhammed's teary eyes sharpened. He now looked like the skilled negotiator and salesman he was.

"Y-yes," she said. "He said he would ask you."

"He has. Both today and before today. I hesitated because he seemed so young and inexperienced. Yet today I remember. I remember I was no older or more experienced when I married your mother. Bring the phone! I must call him and tell him I grant him the greatest gift of all—the hand of my daughter."

"Ullu! Ullu! Ullu!" Myriam trilled in joy.

Muhammed and Myriam insisted I stay until the wedding. I did, giving them the finest camera I could find. *Take a picture of the phoenix, if you can,* I wrote on the card.

After the joy of the wedding and the tears of departure, I flew back to London with my precious frozen blood sample in my carry-on luggage. I did not wish to waste a single drop. I would plan how to use it to revive animals.

After I got my PhD at Cambridge, I returned to study cloning at Case Western Reserve. I realized that I could clone the phoenix from the blood sample. I learned how to isolate the phoenix DNA from its blood and place it into an eagle's egg.

I worried as I warmed the phoenix/eagle egg. I was not sure of the temperature it could take. The eggshell was not rock hard like the phoenix egg. I attached a thermocouple and used a laser beam to candle the egg. The embryo was quiescent. I slowly heated the egg. One twenty. One thirty. One forty. One fifty. The embryo began to move. I kept it at one fifty for a day. Then it burst forth in scarlet-and-gold glory.

I feared it would instinctively fly away. I gathered myrrh and palm ashes for its hatching. The chick was already as large as a macaw as it emerged. It looked at me with intelligent curiosity, but no fear. It ate a hole in the ball of myrrh. It flew to the myrrh bush I kept in a pot, gathered more, and ate it. It doubled in size, to that of a young eagle.

The next day it gathered the eggshell pieces, not the ashes, and put them in the hole it had eaten in the ball of myrrh. It closed up the hole, picked up the ball, and placed it in the potted myrrh bush. The bird flew to the door in the lab, pecked on it, and then looked at me. I opened it.

The phoenix flew down the hall to the nearest window. It pecked at it and looked at me. I opened the exit door with a sigh.

"This is the way out if you wish."

It flew to my shoulder, rubbed its head on my cheek, and then flew out. I watched it fly around the university, then return and land on my shoulder.

This was my first phoenix. I named it Scheherazade. Later, I cloned the second phoenix and bred the two. But that is another story.

This was my first short story. I planned for more stories from my early years in this volume, but they just didn't come to fruition.

Wheels in Time

by Tori Smith

Contents

Prologue

The scene was chaos! I knew immediately I was in a different country, judging by the languages I couldn't understand. I had also determined this was no modern city—I seemed to be on the outskirts of town amid a swarming crowd. Men were shouting and women were crying; meanwhile, I was still trying to figure out how I had gotten there and where exactly I was. Several seconds later, however, that question was answered.

Soldiers were pushing along three men, all in their twenties or thirties, but this was hard to tell because of how worn, bruised, and bloodied they were, seeming to crumple underneath the weight of the large wooden beams they were carrying.

One of the men, seeming weaker than the others, collapsed. The guards did nothing other than yelling at someone in the crowd to help. As the crumpled man staggered to his feet, I saw the twisted wreath of thorns on top of his head. Then I knew the scene, a story I had heard every Easter in varying degrees of detail.

The scene was every bit as horrific as I had been told as I watched the passing of those to be crucified. I was still wondering how I had gotten to this place in history. I looked down at my feet on the scuffed footplates of the old wheelchair—what had happened to my shoes?

1 The Morning Changed Everything!

My adventure began on a normal Monday morning. We were in a hurry because people had overslept and the bus would be there to pick us up in fifteen minutes. For me, being late was never a good thing. I moved slowly, so that didn't go over too well. I had cerebral palsy, but I tried not to let it slow me down much.

"Michael," my mother admonished my brother, "put away the iPad. The bus will be here soon."

My brother groaned but did as he was told.

"Did you finish your homework?" my mother asked.

My brother rolled his eyes. "Yeah, Mom. Geez!"

My brother was fifteen, almost sixteen, though his height made him seem like he was much older. Like my father, he had a slim build with dark hair and features. I was much fairer with lighter hair and skin, though I had a few freckles.

"Bethany, finish your cereal and get downstairs," my mother ordered shortly.

Unlike Michael, I only nodded, shoved my last mouthful of

cereal into my mouth, and began maneuvering my electric wheelchair away from the table and toward the family room to the elevator, which went down to the basement.

My wheelchair, like many of my clothes and other personal items, was a hand-me-down. It had been purchased for $150 from Mrs. Crandall across the street after her husband had passed away. The wheelchair was a little too big for me, though my parents had tried to get a better seat. It was scuffed and dirty, like it had been red at one point, but it was hard to tell now.

The bus was just pulling up when we exited the garage. The bus was small with enough room for a couple of wheelchairs and eight to ten able-bodied passengers. I double-checked my backpack as the driver tied me down. I was feeling slightly better now that I was actually on the bus. Hopefully, I would actually get to school on time.

The ride took no longer than I expected though—the creaking of the bus and the endless chatter of the other students made it seem longer. Finally, the high school came into view. I glanced at the clock on my smartphone, which I would have to put away when the bell rang. It was five to eight; we were cutting it close. I glanced at Michael—not that he cared. He was sitting two seats ahead of me, laughing with one of his friends who also took the number 24 bus. The boys and other passengers headed out of the bus as soon as the door had opened. I shook my head.

I always took school much more seriously than Michael. I was the oldest and not quite eighteen. Thank God I would be graduating soon.

I beat it through the crowd as fast as I could, but usually I got the short end of the stick because people walked in front of me, not even caring I was there. I searched the crowd frantically for my best friend, Carter. We had been friends since grade school and were inseparable.

Finally, I saw Carter heading toward the lockers as the bell rang.

"You're late," he stated, though he didn't look that surprised.

He was pretty average as far as guys went, not as tall as Michael and without a shred of athleticism in his body. He was the self-proclaimed school nerd, and he was cool with that. I was cool with that as long as it meant I had someone to double-check my atrocious math homework. He had sandy-brown hair, offset by striking blue eyes that always sparkled when he laughed.

"Yeah," I replied. "Mom was taking her sleeping pills again."

He nodded as we fell into step with each other—he always slowed down for me. After dumping our stuff in the lockers, we headed for homeroom. Thankfully, we had a few of the same teachers this year.

"You finally got that new chair," Carter mused.

"Well, new to me." I shrugged. "Well, let's just crank up this dinosaur and see if we can actually get to homeroom before the tardy bell rings."

"You want me to jump on the back?" Carter teased.

"With this bucket of bolts? No way! It would probably collapse!"

Laughing, we headed for the classroom at the end of the hall. Unfortunately, I never got there.

2 Lost in Time

When I stopped, I looked around. Instead of being at the end of the hallway in my high school, I was on the side of a long, dusty road amid a shouting crowd, and I had a weird moment, like when Dorothy landed in Oz. I was definitely not in my midwestern high school anymore, or even in what looked like the twenty-first century.

I knew it was futile, but I called anyway. "Carter? Where are you?"

My voice was swallowed up by the din. It didn't seem like anyone knew I was there—either they were too preoccupied with the scene before them, or I couldn't be seen—that, even, in fact, I wasn't sure.

Perplexed, I watched the scene around me. Men were shouting in various languages. I could pick up at least two different ones, though I didn't recognize either. Women were crying, their heads and shoulders wrapped in linen scarves. It was then the soldiers approached. They seemed to be "herding" three young men, ranging from their early twenties to their late thirties, but judging from their bruised and bloodied bodies, it was hard to tell. The little clothes they were wearing seemed to hang on them, and even from where I was, I could see the large gashes that stood out on their backs and shoulders. They were carrying large beams like four-by-fours across their shoulders.

The last man they brought out seemed weaker than the others. He stumbled every few steps and wobbled with the beam across his shoulders. The soldiers seemed to be impatient and stood there with their whips at the ready, not that this man needed them.

When the man finally collapsed barely halfway down the road, one of the soldiers barked at a man nearby to help him carry the heavy wooden beam.

I watched as some of the crowd fell back while others followed along until the guards pushed them back. I stayed where I was. I didn't want to see the execution—it had been depicted enough in movies (with varying degrees of success) for me to know what happened. Then, of course, there were the accounts in the Bible...I knew what happened.

As the crowd dispersed, I moved as carefully as I could.

"Take me back..." I mumbled. "I'm supposed to be in English right now."

Suddenly the wheelchair gave a bump and a jerk, and I thought I had hit a stone. The motor made a noise like SNAP, and I was moving forward again. Everything around me passed in a blur, and I frantically fiddled with the knobs. I still didn't know where I was going.

Finally, when I had a moment to look, I realized I was missing my shoes.

Great, I thought. *I've lost my shoes somewhere in the space-time continuum.* I had never been a big fan of science fiction.

3 Music in the Catacombs

Finally, everything stopped spinning. I looked around. I was pretty sure I was still in the first century, judging from the lack of vehicles and other such technology. The place where I was could best be described as nondescript, dank and dark. Off in the distance, I could hear voices; they were singing.

I seemed to be in a long tunnel, which I continued to follow. It was a shame I didn't have a flashlight, but that wasn't something you needed when you left the house for school in the morning. I followed the voices toward the only light I could see, which was far off in the distance and finally came to a large cavern where several people were gathered, many of them around tables. Like the rest of the furnishings, everything was crude, scuffed, and dusty.

Several faces looked up, and when they saw me around the corner, their eyes widened and small children hid behind their mothers. They reminded me of a pack of curious puppies as they looked bemused. Some of the men approached, a couple of them with swords raised cautiously. They were speaking in a language I didn't understand, so I did my best to look harmless.

They circled me several times and tapped the wheelchair, confused by the advanced technology.

Finally I spoke, hesitantly and slowly. "I mean you no harm. I'm lost"—I knew they would never fully understand my real predicament—"and I need to know where I am."

Then a woman of indeterminable age rushed forward. She could have been anywhere from her late thirties to early sixties, and like the rest of the group, she had a worn look about her.

She spoke to the men, who still looked confused. I could tell, even not knowing her words, that she was exasperated. Then she spoke to me, and despite neither of us understanding, I got the gist of what she was saying. I could stay—this place was open to anyone who needed shelter.

I knew the group was hiding, but I didn't say I knew from what; that would be more perplexing still. They were hiding from the terror of the Roman city above them. These were the first Christians—the early church. Back then the church was the people and not just a building. It would be many centuries before the church would be a building, let alone an organization.

I made my place at one of the tables and still felt uncomfortable around these strange people; I was equally strange to them. "My name is Bethany. I don't know what I'm doing here, and I know we don't understand each other. You can't even begin to understand what I've been through."

Finally one of the younger men spoke. "Bethany...you believe...ichthus?"

I knew very little Greek, just a few words mentioned in weekend sermons. I only nodded. This was going to take some explaining.

After a meal of some bland stew one of the women had cooked, I pulled out my phone. The people seemed interested; they had never seen anything like it before.

"It does all sorts of things," I explained slowly. "I can talk to other people, take pictures, and play music." Even those things took several minutes to explain. To demonstrate, I played one of my favorite songs by British singer-songwriter Ed Sheeran.

The people looked confused, as rightly they should be, but then they nodded their heads, and a few smiled. I tried to steer clear of the few of the songs I knew had cuss words in them; that probably wouldn't go over too well once I explained it. I grinned to myself.

I turned up my iPhone as loud as it would go. The catacombs provided great acoustics, but the modern sounds echoed eerily in the long, twisting tunnels. I chose from my favorite contemporary Christian music (as the music had been categorized since the early '80s)—Newsboys, Mandisa, and several others popular on the radio in 2018. As the music began, I explained that while my music was a little "different," it served the same purpose, to bring honor and glory to God. That was something they understood.

After the singing and dancing to the various music (theirs and mine) had wound down, everyone began to settle in for the night. The young children went to bed on pallets in dark corners, their mothers singing softly, covering them with blankets. I watched this for a while, until even the young men, some no older than I was, had settled down. I waited till everyone was asleep, then moved to the other side of the large room. I set everything in motion, hoping I was headed in the right direction to get home. I heard the now-familiar SNAP, and I was off, leaving the catacombs behind.

I was relieved when I saw the familiar hallways of my high school. Apparently little time had passed with my jumps in time back to the first century. When I entered my first-hour classroom, Carter was already sitting down.

"Where have you been?" he whispered. "What happened? I thought you were right behind me!"

Long story, I mouthed as I pulled my supplies out on my wheelchair desk. Under the guise of listening to our teacher's lecture, I told him what happened.

4 Passing Notes

Keeping one ear on the teacher's lecture on the latest chapter of *The Crucible* (snore), I told Carter what had happened. We passed the notes back and forth old school, but it was the only way I could explain what had happened. I only hoped we didn't get caught. I wasn't that type of student, and neither was Carter.

What happed?-C

I think I went back in time. To the first century to be exact-B

When? How-C

To biblical time. I saw the crucifixion.-B

You saw the crucifixion?-C

Not exactly... I mean, I didn't stay for it. As soon as things got crazy I got out of there.-B

Then what?-C

I think I was in ancient Rome... When the Christians were hiding... You know, the early first century and all that.-B

So you went back in time? How?-C

I don't know...-B

I scribbled, trying to think of the best way to describe it.

I think it's the wheelchair-B

Your wheelchair is a time machine? You realize how crazy that sounds!-C

I know! But it just happened...-B

Then I filled him in on what happened when I was there

with the early Christians in the catacombs, about the evening I had spent there before I had come back home.

You introduced them to Ed Sheeran? That's crazy!-C

And contemporary Christian music-B

You're nuts!-C

Gee, thanks for noticing-B

I wished you could write sarcasm.

This all sounds like a bad science fiction novel. You got to show me all this later.-C

Count on it!-B

* * *

While waiting for the bus, I showed Carter how it worked. With my luck, we would be back by the time the bus came... I hoped.

Carter frowned.

"Okay..."

"Just stand on the back and hold on tight."

Carter raised his eyebrows.

"Fine, but if this thing collapses, it's not my fault."

I started driving slowly at first, then faster and faster when I wasn't sure how fast I was going. I heard the telltale SNAP, and we were off. I hoped Carter was still behind me.

It seemed we had only gone a few feet and we were back in my kitchen, as it had been that morning. I was now looking at myself and my brother eating breakfast.

"How?" Carter whispered.

"Don't know," I replied. "I still don't know what triggers it."

"Right. I've seen it," Carter replied firmly. "Let's just get back to school and head home. This time at the proper time."

I focused my attention exactly eight hours later as I turned the wheelchair, hoping I ended up in the right place again.

5 Dragons!

So Carter and I returned to school—or what we thought

was the school in 2018. We arrived in the soccer field next to the school, but there was something different about it. There seemed to be fewer buildings and not a soul in sight.

When I turned to look for Carter, he was gone.

Uh-oh. That wasn't good.

The only thing I saw was a little old lady crossing the street, seemingly in a hurry. She was dressed in blue and white and was wearing a bonnet and an apron, out of place for the twenty-first century.

Before I twiddled the knobs on my wheelchair again, I looked around. This time I spotted something in the sky. At first I thought it was a bird of prey, an eagle or a hawk. But when I looked again, I saw that it was something much bigger! Actually, it was three somethings that appeared to be dragons.

I shook my head at the brilliant-blue sky.

There was no such thing as a dragon.

I watched as they landed. It appeared to be a mated pair with a youngster. They were shades of orange, blue, and gray, with something vaguely doggish about their features, but something definitely reptilian. They didn't seem to be hostile. They looked at me, as interested as cows grazing in a field.

While the female groomed her youngster, the male wandered over to me, sniffing curiously, making a low rumbling noise.

"And I wonder how I ended up here," I muttered. "Have you seen Carter? Or did he get lost sometime between here and seven thirty a.m.?"

The male made another low growl and looked at me placidly with cool green eyes.

"I'll be back—I hope," I murmured. "Right now I have to find my best friend...and my shoes."

There was nothing like bopping through the space-time continuum in just your socks.

6 Back to the Beginning

So I retraced my steps. First, I went back to the scene at breakfast—no Carter. I certainly wasn't going to ask my mother. The time traveling stuff was weird enough. There was no point in freaking her out.

From there, I went directly into the time stream, which I normally wouldn't have done because that's where people get lost and split in half and stuff like that (at least according to fantasy and science fiction). At the moment, I had no idea exactly where I was going, but I knew I was going forward, back to the present. He had to be somewhere.

The time stream was interesting. It was a mass of swirling blue and white, and at various intervals, there were doors timestamped with years. It was at one of these posts I saw Carter. He was holding on for dear life and looked like a stranded hitchhiker.

I grinned when I saw him.

Carter only scowled. "Took you long enough," he grumbled. "You didn't even notice I fell off!"

"Well, unless you want to end up in ancient Rome again, time traveling takes concentration!" I shot back.

I waited until he climbed onto the back of the wheelchair.

"If you must know, I did get lost. I ended up in some future dimension with dragons."

When I looked back at him, he was frowning.

"Dragons? Where the heck did you end up, Beth?"

I shrugged as I turned around, heading back toward 3:30 p.m.

"I'll have to take you there sometime," I reflected. "These dragons, at least the ones I met, were really friendly. They were kind of like big dogs."

Carter gave a short laugh. "I'll believe that when I see it. I think we've had enough time travel for today, and we have a lot of questions to answer."

Finally, we returned to where the buses were waiting.

"I'll see you tomorrow." Carter waved as he headed toward his bus. Then he turned and frowned again, looking at me, his blue eyes puzzled.

"Hey, Beth, where are your shoes? You had them this morning."

"You tell me," I replied. "I think I lost them somewhere between here and the first century."

7 Pressing Questions

A few days later, I found Carter pacing my bedroom in a businesslike way.

"At this rate, you're going to wear a hole in my carpet," I responded dryly.

"Well, do you want to figure this out?"

"Sure I do, but I never thought I'd be in the middle of something like this. It's like straight out of Nancy Drew or something."

"What about your shoes, Bethany?" Carter asked. "Shoes just don't disappear."

I sighed. "Well, add that to the list then."

Carter stopped pacing and walked over to my desk and wrote something on a piece of paper. Then he came back to me and showed me what he had written.

On top of the paper he had written: *Weird Stuff That Has Happened with Bethany's Wheelchair.*

Then he made some sort of table. In one column he wrote *incident*, and in the other column he wrote *questions*.

In each of the columns he had written down several events and the following questions:

Bethany loses shoes—what happened to the shoes? (Somewhere in the first century).

Wheelchair goes back in time—why? (This had been an arrow pointed toward the top of the paper, suggesting it should be the first question.)

What determines time travel?

Where did the wheelchair come from? How did it become a time machine?

I pointed to the last question.

"That's two questions, and I told you it came from my neighbor."

"That doesn't answer the question about how it became a time machine," Carter argued. "People just don't build time machines. That stuff only happens in sci-fi."

I smirked. "Or so you think."

When Carter left a few hours later, I was compiling my own list. Things I wanted to experiment with the time machine. I wanted to see if I could return to the places I had found by accident. I wanted to see if I could go into my own future because I wanted to see where Carter and I ended up. I was seriously curious to see if we ended up dating, but I wasn't going to tell him that. Above all, however, I needed to find if I could get to the place in biblical times where I had lost my shoes.

It seemed Carter and I had a lot of questions to answer.

While I contemplated what Carter and I had discussed, I decided to talk to my mother about the wheelchair (in present time, mind you—the time travel stuff would freak her out). I finally managed to talk to her before dinner the following day, before my dad and Michael came in. If I said anything about my suspicions and what I wanted to know in front of them, I would never hear the end of it.

"Hey, Mom, can I talk to you about something?"

"Sure, dear," my mother replied as she was cleaning the chicken to be put on the grill in the next half hour.

"Well, it's about my wheelchair. It seems to be acting funny."

My mother frowned. "How so?"

I paused, then reframed my inquiry. "Do you know where Mrs. Crandall got the wheelchair for her husband?"

"No," my mother replied mildly. "All she said was he had done some 'customization,' whatever that means. Why?"

"I thought she might have a better idea of why it acts the way it does."

Pausing, I again rephrased what I was thinking. "Carter and I have some suspicions about the wheelchair. It's been acting really strange."

My mother paused in her act of cleaning the chicken. "Strange how? Mrs. Crandall assured me it was in good working condition, at least until we can buy you your own. Why didn't you tell me you were having problems?"

Now she sounded like my mom.

I shifted in my seat uncomfortably.

"Well, it's not those kinds of problems. I mean, not the kind a tech guy can fix."

My mother raised her eyebrows, her grimy hands still suspended over the raw chicken.

At that point, I figured I was too far in and decided to go for broke. I told her everything that had happened since I had started school that year, and as I'd suspected, she looked skeptical. I mean, how else would your mother look if you told her your wheelchair was a time machine?

For a long time, as she continued to prepare dinner, she didn't say anything. I could almost *hear* her thinking. Finally, she replied stiffly, "I agree that you should talk to Mrs. Crandall. I'm sure she'll be more than happy to answer any questions."

I nodded, satisfied. "Thanks, Mom. I'll ask her this weekend. I still have English homework to finish after dinner."

Just then Michael came up the stairs. He seemed to have overheard the last of my comment.

"You waiting till after dinner to finish homework? I think I might faint!" He responded sarcastically.

I resisted the urge to roll my eyes. It was times like this I put on my older-sister hat. "Well, I really don't want to be perusing ten encyclopedias before I go to bed," I retorted. "After a while, everything blurs together, and unless I want my last few paragraphs on Shakespeare to be garbage, I'll do it while I'm thinking straight, thank you!" I said this all without missing a beat before Michael had even sat down.

Before Michael could reply, my father appeared. He had a beer in one hand and the day's mail in the other.

"Daniel, you can start the grill in fifteen minutes," my mother told him as she rinsed her hands in the sink.

My father made a noise that he had heard her and understood and then sat down with the mail. In the meantime, I turned my attention to my impending homework. I had so much to tell Carter tomorrow, he was going to freak! Meanwhile, I figured I would run a few "experiments."

8 Test 1: Back to the Future

I decided to hold off on talking to Mrs. Crandall, as there were other things I wanted to do first. My first test was to see if I could (on purpose) go to my own future. If that wasn't something straight out of science fiction, I didn't know what was.

I planned the trip for Saturday morning, when I would have time to experiment and could go farther without being interrupted.

I decided to go someplace where I wouldn't be observed, and if I happened to disappear, it would go unnoticed.

I headed to the park by my house, or at least in the general direction. At some point, I slipped into the time stream, and everything was a blur. I didn't know exactly where I was going, but I knew "when" I wanted to go. By now I had figured out the general idea of going through time had to do with the joystick and how far the seat was tilted back, which was controlled by the knob at the base of the seat. I tried for ten years in the future (I thought twenty would be too many). My main concern was getting stuck and not being able to find my way back again.

Finally, when everything stopping spinning, I looked around. I was in a different house, an apartment. I could see myself talking on the phone. Even without knowing the details, I knew I was talking to Carter. Then the scene dissolved as time shifted around me.

I saw another scene. We were at one of our favorite places, having coffee (nothing new there). We were talking quietly, our heads close together. Afterward, we left together and drove somewhere else. I followed since I could, and I was not bound by the loop of time while I observed.

We were walking in a local park that seemed to be the very one I had been heading for in the present time, only the trees were much older. It seemed to be fall instead of early summer, and by now it was growing dark. I could barely see the two figures ahead of me. The future Carter and Bethany were talking so quietly, I could barely hear them, even from where I observed. They were nothing more than shadows.

We seemed very close, closer than friends, I thought, but I wasn't going to get my hopes up. After all, the future could always change. Carter stroked my face, brushing my hair out of my eyes. My future self was gripping his arm, looking up at him.

Then future Carter leaned down and kissed future Bethany. We were definitely dating, but seeming to take it slow, as I knew Carter would. I shifted the knobs and dials on my wheelchair, sighing as I looked back at the scene one last time. That was what I needed to know.

For now, Carter didn't need to know I had "cheated" the time thing and why. It wasn't time for that yet.

9 Test 2: Valley of Big Dogs

"You want to go where?" Carter asked when I saw him the following Monday.

I dropped my voice to a whisper. "I want to see if I can find the dragons again. I told you I would show you."

"Fine," Carter replied. "We can go during study hall. We got all the time in the world, right?" He grinned.

My stomach fluttered, but I ignored it. I still hadn't told him about my *other* trip, though I had mentioned I was doing some experiments with where I could go and when.

I was anxious about the impending trip most of the morning, though I tried to keep my attention on my schoolwork. At this point, I was glad this was my last year and that I would be graduating in a few weeks. For now, it was buckle-down time, though I was convinced junior year had been harder. Usually, the last semester of senior year was a breeze.

Over study hall, Cater and I put our plan into action. If I played my cards right, I could freeze time long enough to get out without being noticed, and we would be back before anyone knew we were gone.

At some point, I knew Carter had made an excuse to get away, and I made the pretense of going to get a drink of water. A few minutes later, we met in the deserted hallway by the back doors.

"Don't think you can get me to make it a habit of playing hooky," Carter commented as we made our way outside. Technically, we weren't even going off school property.

I smirked.

"That depends on how you define playing hooky."

"As long as I'm back in enough time to study for calculus and trig."

I rolled my eyes.

By now I knew what I was doing, although I didn't know how it was done. I was still surprised the wheelchair held up to Carter standing on the back, but it was no ordinary wheelchair.

I figured the dimension I was going to was just a "shift" in time. Dimensions seemed to be easier to navigate than certain time periods, since they were essentially on the same wavelength as the present time, simply in a different location. The idea we discussed a lot was how no one noticed we were gone and for how long. I determined the jump in the time stream caused time to temporarily freeze, and we were dropped off coming and going as if no time had passed in our own time. That came in handy, so we didn't have to always explain where we had been.

After what seemed like only a few seconds, we were in the field again. This time Carter was with me. I let out a sigh of relief.

After several minutes, I saw the dragons coming. As before, they flew in groups, either families or couples. There were few lone dragons, and the groups of families and mated couples seemed to have seniority over the loners.

After several minutes, I spotted the family I had seen before, the blue male and red-orange female. The youngster had grown, and the female seemed carried something on her back.

Carter looked surprised. "Wow! Beth, this is incredible! At least they're friendly."

"So far," I muttered as the male approached me, made a snuffling noise, and gave me another critical glance before turning back to his family.

When his head swung toward me again, I tentatively reached out my hand and rubbed the large forehead. The luminous eyes closed, and the dragon made a purring-like noise.

"Do you know if they breathe fire?" Carter asked. "What's a dragon that doesn't breathe fire?"

I shrugged. Just then I noticed the female and what she was carrying. She was closer today than before, less wary. There, close beside her, was a new baby, likely only a few weeks old. Grayish in color and fuzzy around the face and shoulders, it didn't have the bright colors of the older dragons. Its large, luminous eyes seemed too big for its face. The baby stared blearily out of blue-gray irises.

The female made some sort of nest and eventually plopped in the baby dragon, which let out a squawking birdlike whine. Then the mother bent her head and blew a flame around the nest, causing it to smolder and simmer.

I turned to Carter.

"Well, apparently they do breathe fire."

* * *

Several days had passed since our excursion to see the dragons. Carter had even joked we were now qualified to officially learn "how to train a dragon."

"So what are you going to do now?" Carter asked as we spent yet another Sunday afternoon discussing our time travel plans.

"I think it's time we go back to the beginning," I replied.

"Does that mean what I think it does?" Carter asked.

"I think it's time we find my shoes. I want you to come with me."

10 The Woman in Red

Carter and I planned our trip back to the first century carefully. We planned like we were going on an extended trip, filling our backpacks accordingly.

Amid all that, we were also preparing for graduation, ordering our caps and gowns for the ceremony, but I was sure everything would be resolved before then. Time was on our side (ha-ha). I still had to talk to Mrs. Crandall, and Carter had to practice his valedictorian speech. Of course, we could do none of that until we got back, which would be an undertaking in itself.

We planned the trip for the weekend before graduation. Lately, we had been too busy to do a quick trip. Besides, this would take two or three days on the other end, and I wanted to give it the time it deserved since it might take a while to find my shoes. It might seem like going back two thousand years was a long way just to find a pair of shoes, but they were one of the few pairs I could wear that accommodated small, spastic feet. I might have had other pairs, but the blue and green ones were my favorite.

"We look like we're running away from home," Carter commented a few days before we were to leave.

I laughed as I shoved a sweater into my backpack. "Yeah, no kidding. You'll bring food and water, won't you, nonperishable, of course? It may take us a bit to retrace my steps. I was outside of town when I lost them."

Carter nodded. "Yeah, I thought of that." He grinned, "Got you covered, Beth."

"Good," I replied. "I guess I'll see you this weekend."

"And tomorrow, and the day after that, and the day after that..." Carter responded, laughing.

I threw a pillow at him as he walked out of the door, which, of course, missed horribly.

Carter and I departed from behind the school that Saturday morning. I tried following roughly the same path I had followed the first time, which was kind of hard because I was coming from a different angle (so to speak).

When I opened my eyes again, we appeared to be somewhere outside Jerusalem. I could see the city in the distance, and at the moment no one was around.

"Where did we end up?" Carter asked as he slid off the back off my wheelchair. "Before or after the crucifixion?"

"After, I think..." I glanced down at a dial on the chair, which had spat out a series of numbers. "I'd still be careful going into town. I don't know what these Roman soldiers are going to do. It's like bad political backlash."

Carter chuckled under his breath. Then he shouldered our packs as we made our way toward the city.

Aside from normal day-to-day activities, the streets were sparse. Travelers were common in Jerusalem even back then, so no one really paid us much attention, even to our other-time dress, and my wheelchair seemed to be shielded somehow.

"So where do we start?" I asked Carter. "No one's going to know what size 3 Toms slip-ons look like."

"Well," Carter began, "we're travelers. Someone should offer us a place to stay, food, and all that."

The houses seem to be worked into the very walls themselves. Some were even hidden, going into upper rooms but had no entrance from the street itself.

We were headed toward the center of the city and were about halfway (trying to stay away from the soldiers as much as possible) when we saw a woman in the doorway of one of the houses. She waved at us, apparently indicating we should come in. She was small, with dark Middle Eastern features. The most notable thing about her appearance was her red headscarf, which covered most of her face.

I noticed a predicament. It was the first time I had really looked around the city, and I realized most of the houses were on multiple levels with stairs in between, like some sort of ancient apartment complex. Clearly not handicapped accessible.

"Uh-oh," I muttered to Carter, "how am I going to get up there?"

Carter followed my gaze, frowned, then turned back to me. "I'll make quick introductions and take our packs, then I'll come back for you."

I watched as he hurried up the stone steps and conversed with the woman. They were both gesturing, if only to make up a lack of understanding. Finally, he came back down, his face tight.

"I gather we can stay, though I know she doesn't understand what we're doing or why we're here." He shrugged. "Which is just as well."

"So are you going to carry me or what?" I asked bluntly.

Carter sighed. He still looked stressed, like the trip was more than he'd bargained for.

"What choice do I have?" He chuckled under his breath, then grinned in a self-deprecating way.

Several awkward moments later, we were in the small, cramped house. (The time machine had been hidden as best as Carter could hide it, in a deserted corner under a discarded piece of fabric that looked like it had been a cloak at one point). I had been relegated to a pallet on the floor since I couldn't really sit in a chair. The woman by now understood I was disabled—that much was obvious. I was beginning to understand the plight of disabled people in third-world countries, that they weren't really part of things and it was enough to keep them alive.

Finally, everyone seemed to be on the same page. The woman had figured we were travelers, judging by our packs. Carter had even gotten her name: Rahab.

Rahab asked where we were from, and Carter fabricated some answer. I felt weird talking in front of her in English. It felt like we were having two separate conversations, but Carter pulling out a smartphone with a translation app probably wasn't a good idea. We talked quietly while Rahab served us, and we showed her we were grateful the best we could. (I was served on the pallet on the floor, though I made the best of it). The situation was every bit as awkward as I could have imagined.

Sometime later Carter and I were settled down on pallets on the other side of the main room. Once Rahab had gone to bed, we talked in low whispers.

"Are you going to ask her about the shoes?"

"I don't know yet," Carter muttered. "Obviously the internet doesn't work here, and I don't know enough Aramaic to describe them."

"Do you think someone picked them up and tried to sell them?" I asked.

"It's possible," Carter murmured. "We can always look around the market in the morning."

This was agreed on as we settled down, while my brain worked away about how we were going to function in the here and now.

11 To Market

Carter and I woke early the next morning. The sun was still rising, and there was a glow in the sky. Could you get jet lagged from time travel?

We ate a breakfast of lentils with herbs and dried fruit, then Rahab, Carter, and I left for the local market and Carter, and I executed the plan we had discussed the night before. Carter would retrieve my hidden wheelchair, and though moving through the narrow, dusty streets would be tricky, it would be better than trying to negotiate steps. As long as I stayed to the main road, I would be okay. Still, it was not an ideal situation for someone who was disabled.

"Are you sure you don't want me to carry you?" Carter looked at me sideways as we prepared to leave the house, though I was still set on using the wheelchair. "We still run the risk of people asking too many questions."

Finally, I caved. No matter what century I was in, I valued my independence, and giving it up was something of a fail.

"Fine! Ask Rahab. See if she has any suggestions."

Sometime after breakfast I was strapped to Carter's back

like a big baby. It was the best thing we could come up with since Rahab seemed slightly confused as to why I didn't want to stay at the house. I couldn't explain to her that after our excursion, we had to get back to our own time.

I groaned as Carter began jogging awkwardly. It was going to be a long morning.

Between perusing the items vendors had for sale (we had no local currency), we searched for where my shoes might have disappeared to. The market, like everything else, was tight, and it took all my effort not to knock anything over or scare the living daylights out of passing livestock.

Finally after hours of searching, for this was easier said than done because the market was crowded both with animals and people, we found my shoes at the stall of a textile merchant. He was a thin man who looked slightly unwell, with short dark hair under his head wrap, elongated features (this included his nose and earlobes), and a wheezy-sounding voice. He might have been no older than Carter and I were, but this era and environment did not treat him well. I was reminded that people in biblical times barely lived past fifty, if that.

Carter talked fast (even in garbled Aramaic), but it was something he was good at—negotiating. The merchant finally agreed to give us the shoes in exchange for something else, and after several minutes of discussion, we sold one of our knapsacks (it was a good knapsack). It would serve someone well, given it was machine made in the twenty-first century.

"You know what today is?" Carter muttered under his breath.

I frowned at him.

"It's Sunday. Jesus is risen." He looked around cautiously. "I keep hearing Peter's name pop up here and there. My guess is the disciples are all lying low somewhere. Well, we know it's true." He gave me a conspiratorial grin.

I grinned back.

We planned to leave as soon as possible, as there was no point in hanging around and explaining ourselves if we didn't have to.

After one last meal with Rahab, Carter relayed our excuses to Rahab, and she nodded. Clearly she had dealt with travelers before.

"She says, 'Safe journey,'" Carter translated.

"Well, tell her thank you," I replied. "We appreciate it."

Carter and I had decided we better get going before dark. It was going to be harder to navigate then, even if we had some light to work by. The light from the chair wouldn't be enough.

We packed our items into our one remaining knapsack, which Carter carried, then we headed back. I was shooting for sometime on Sunday afternoon—that way it wouldn't look like we had been gone for almost a day and a half. We returned to the exact same spot we had left, then headed home, back to my house, where Carter's car was parked in my parents' driveway.

"Thank God we're back in the twenty-first century," I quipped. "I think I've had all the stew and lentils I want for a while."

Carter chuckled. "Yeah, I know what you mean."

Before I headed inside (the garage door was still open, so I was able to get my wheelchair into the house), I gave Carter a quick hug goodbye.

"See you on Monday," I said shortly. "Then it's back to graduation practice."

Carter grinned. "Yeah, I guess so. I hope no one asks how we spent our weekend. It's going to be a little hard to explain. Oh, here are you shoes, Beth. I don't you want to forget them again."

"Hey, at least they're in this century," I replied, laughing.

We waved at each other as Carter ducked into his car. I watched until the car had disappeared around the corner.

My mother was in the kitchen when I came in.

"Did you have a nice walk?" she asked. "I hope it's not getting too hot out there."

"We had a nice time, and no, it's not too bad out there yet," I replied. Then I headed for my room. It was high time I got out of my wheelchair.

12 Matter of Time

It was the week after graduation. Going into summer, it was everything you'd expect—sunny, perfect temperatures (for now), and no one had gotten bored yet. Despite preparing for our impending future, many of my friends were taking some free time, one last summer before reality as adults kicked in.

I felt like I owed myself a little. I had worked hard the last four years. I was going to the community college in the fall, so at least for the next few months, I could take it easy. I knew Carter already had his college lined up. He had his next four years planned out, and his future was much more detailed than mine. While college loomed somewhere off in the distance, I had other mysteries to solve.

Carter and I had breezed out of school the evening of graduation with a quick "see you tomorrow," which I knew we would since we would probably spend most of the summer together until he left for college. At the moment, I didn't even want to think about Carter leaving. It would be like losing an arm or some other useful appendage.

My goal so far was to solve the mystery of my time traveling wheelchair. That answer happened to be across the street, where Mrs. Crandall lived and could be seen every day from the front window of my house, watering her hydrangeas, which were so numerous. Everyone joked they would most likely take over the world.

Mrs. Crandall was the type of woman people tended to underestimate. She would have been described as small but mighty. Though in her seventies, she looked much younger. A spry, short woman with short white hair who was kind to everybody and was the person who always had the best treats on Halloween (according to the neighborhood kids)—that was the type of person she was.

"So do you want to come?" I asked Carter.

He shrugged. "Sure, why not? Best she hears it from both of us, I think."

A short time later, we were standing on Mrs. Crandall's lawn. (Well, me, I was sitting, as usual.)

Mrs. Crandall was confused when she saw Carter at first, since they had never spoken. However, when she saw me, she smiled. "Bethany, I assume this young man is a friend of yours."

I nodded, and Carter introduced himself. I was sure she had seen him around more than once from across the street.

"So nice to see you. It's been a while. Your folks doing okay?"

"They're fine, thank you," I replied. "Mrs. Crandall, we

came to see you because we had a few questions about this wheelchair. It's been acting a bit...strangely."

Mrs. Crandall didn't look surprised, only thoughtful. "Carter, is it?" she asked. "Why don't you get the old ramp from the garage and come on in, both of you. I think I have some information that may be of use to you."

Sometime later, after much maneuvering and with the help of an ancient ramp that looked like it had once belonged in the Middle Ages, Carter and I were in Mrs. Crandall's living room.

"So what's been going on with my husband's old chair?" she asked, though I had a feeling she already knew the answer.

Taking turns, though Carter and I had the habit of finishing each other's sentences, we told Mrs. Crandall what had been happening. She listened patiently. Then after we had finished, she finally spoke, a soft smile curling her thin mouth.

"Matthew always did like to tinker with things," she mused.

Carter and I looked at each other, exchanging one of our best-friend looks that said we knew exactly what the other person was thinking.

"He always did like that science stuff and math I never understood, even back then." She smiled again, but she looked sad.

That sounded exactly like Carter, a class nerd.

"Well, about ten or fifteen years ago, he decided he wanted to build a time machine of some sort. He said it had been in his back pocket for years, but he had never figured out how. I'd find him on Sundays in the garage, when I thought he was taking a nap, but he was stubborn right up to the end, so he kept messing around with things. Until one day I couldn't find him. He had completely disappeared from the garage. I knew he hadn't gone far, as he couldn't move that fast to begin with. Then he returned what seemed to be an hour later ranting about the Renaissance, da Vinci, and van Gogh. He said he had done it, though it was rough and unpredictable. The system wasn't quite worked out yet. It had 'bugs,' in it, as you kids say."

Carter spoke first. "So that's all it is? Something he was experimenting with and wasn't quite finished with?"

Mrs. Crandall shrugged. "You could say that. That is,

unless you want to finish it?"

Carter gave a short laugh and shook his head. "I'm good with math, science, physics, and stuff like that, but I think that's beyond me."

"I can give you his notes if you would like. That may help with what you have described to me, but the mechanisms and other such little fiddle-faddle would have to be tinkered with to work as Matthew intended."

Despite his earlier intentions, Carter spent the next few weeks trying to get whatever ran the time machine to be more efficient. He poured over Matthew Crandall's notes and consulted his father's books on physics, though much of what he was looking for defied physics or any such science humanity knew of.

One day a few weeks later, Carter did a test run. We were in a deserted parking lot next to a street with minimal traffic so we wouldn't be too obvious.

"You ready for this, Bethany?" he asked as he studied the readout on the joystick from over my shoulder.

I gave him a look. "As ready as I'll ever be," I replied, still slightly apprehensive.

Carter twiddled a few knobs and punched a button. "Okay, go! Go, go, go!" He sounded like a sports coach.

So I went, slowly picking up speed. Then there was the telltale SNAP! And I knew the chair had jumped. Several minutes later I could see and hear a rain forest. Several seconds after that it began to rain. Within that short amount of time, the chair jumped again—mercifully, back to my driveway.

"Does that answer your question about whether it works or not?" I responded crossly. "It sent me into a rain forest and well..." I gestured to my appearance. "You're lucky nothing shorted!"

"The thing that does the time jumps is still unstable, and the thing that stabilizes the duration of the time there is iffy," Carter replied, frowning.

"Brilliant deduction, Einstein," I muttered.

"It still needs work, and the mechanics in the joystick need to be recalibrated. Again." Carter ran a hand through his hair.

"You think this will be ready by the fall?" I asked.

"Likely," Carter grunted, "but not guaranteed. Tinkering

with this thing on top of everything else I have going on may take me the rest of the summer."

"What am I going to do without you?" I asked. I meant the question to be rhetorical, but Carter answered anyway.

"Well, you can always pop around and come see me."

"Which brings me back to my original question," I continued. "No time travel unless this thing is working at least better. Right now it's running like one of those old vintage cars my dad is always talking about."

"Right." Carter sighed, scratched the back of his head, and finally stood up. "We've got almost three months. I'll figure it out. So no time jumps until the mechanism that controls it is at least stable. We both agree it can be a bit unpredictable. I can only guess where you would end up." He chuckled and grinned.

Those three months went way too fast. Before I knew it, Carter was packing for college and intending to leave before classes had even started, to find his dorm, roommate, and what he would do before he ever had to worry about homework.

"It's okay, Beth. We'll keep in touch. There's always text and email. I'll call when I have time, and we have other options." He gave me a sideways smile.

I nodded, still feeling massively out of my element. I was going to have my own adjusting to do. College was a completely different ball game.

Shortly before Thanksgiving, things didn't seem so bad. It had only been a few months, but I was happy. I was at a community college a few miles from home, though I still missed Carter every day. We emailed between classes, and I told him about my homework and dilemmas with my professors.

Hey, come on down before you go home, he suggested in one email. *Maybe we can study together. My campus has this great outdoor quad area.*

Easy for you to say, I wrote back. *You're in North Carolina. I'm still in the snow belt freezing my butt off!*

I went anyway.

I focused my mind on Carter and where I knew he was, and then I "casually" slipped off campus during my lunch break. (I wondered how coffee time traveled).

When the spinning and blurriness from the time stream had cleared, there was Carter in the most clichéd college campus of all time, with the fall leaves settling around him, though it was still quite warm for November.

He smiled. "Hey, you make it okay?"

"As well as to be expected," I replied. "Besides, I didn't really time travel. It was more of a teleport. You're lucky that stabilizer is actually working decently now."

"You got your stuff?" he asked. "I got us a table over there."

"Yeah," I replied, "and I got coffee and cookies, if you want them."

Carter's blue eyes brightened. "Sure! Don't think I can say no to that."

We studied for a while, long enough to get something done and long enough to talk. The coffee and cookies disappeared, and soon we were hugging each other goodbye.

"You heading home after this?" Carter asked.

I nodded. "I know Thanksgiving isn't until next week," I answered, "but it'll be nice to have a real break."

"I'll be headed home pretty soon too," Carter replied, "so you'll see me soon enough."

I beamed, a smile he returned.

Then I turned around and headed back up the path the way I had come. I spared myself one last look back before the chair jumped in the time stream and it was too blurry to see anything, and not for the last time, Carter disappeared from view.

Tori Smith is another new author. She blogs, vlogs, and writes online fiction. Her story is another accidental discovery that makes many surprising turns.

Beginning of Zombie Turkeys related stories

In a Pickle

by Andy Zach

Now, what was he going to do? Brice Butterworth's boss just told him to double the productivity of Vegan Inc.'s pickle strain they used for their Kilwowski Pickle brand. That was completely impossible.

But keeping his job required it. He was the low man on the genetic engineering totem pole at Vegan Inc., the last one hired and the first one to be fired if another recession hit.

He couldn't think. He couldn't face this. So he cruised the internet. "The origin of zombie turkeys? I didn't know they'd found that. Hmm, a *Midley Beacon* exclusive, the foremost zombie news source," he read out loud.

Zombie turkeys had ravaged Illinois and the US at Thanksgiving. Thankfully, they hadn't hit near Terre Haute, where he lived. He skimmed the article rapidly. Corn-All, one of Vegan Inc.'s agribusiness rivals, had genetically modified their corn to fight off corn disease. The genetic modification would adapt to the disease at a cellular level and neutralize it by copying the DNA from the diseased organism, whether fungal or bacteria.

When wild turkeys ate the corn, it modified the E. coli in their gut, creating the zombie turkey bacteria, E. coli Gallopavo. That moved into the turkeys' bloodstream and made them zombies, able to regenerate any lost or damaged body part, even bringing turkeys back from the dead.

What caught Brice's eye was the reproduction rate: zombie cells reproduced every twenty minutes. Could that work for pickles? Why not try?

He read the article more carefully and found it sourced

from a Dr. Edwin Galloway of the Northwestern Poultry Institute. He followed the link to Dr. Galloway's original paper.

There it was. The whole DNA sequence of Corn-All's modification and the zombie turkey bacteria, E. coli Gallopavo. Now, he just needed a sample. Nothing like going to the source. He called Dr. Galloway.

"Hello? Dr. Galloway? This is Brice Butterworth with Vegan Inc."

"Hello, Mr. Butterworth. How can I help you?"

"I read your paper on E. coli Gallopavo, and I'd like to test it on various vegetables. Could I get a sample?"

"I can send you a sample, but the bacteria only affects turkeys, not plants."

"But Corn-All used the sequence in corn."

"Yes, but the zombie effect only showed up in turkeys. E. coli is an animal-specific bacteria."

"No other animals?"

"We only tested turkeys, pigs, chickens, and cows."

"I'll test some other animals."

"All right. I'll send you some of the bacteria and some of the Corn-All corn. Let me know what you find out."

"Will do. Make it a next-day shipment. Vegan Inc. will pay. We're under a time crunch."

"I'll ship it today."

"Thanks so much! This may help solve a problem for me."

"Great! Let me know your results. Be sure to give the Poultry Institute of Northwestern credit."

"You've got it. Bye."

Brice spent the rest of the day thinking about how to get the zombie growth bacteria to grow in the pickles. Maybe he could genetically engineer them so they appeared to be turkeys to the bacteria? That would be a kind of chimera, a hybrid between turkey and cucumber. He went out and bought a pair of live turkeys from eTurkey, the online turkey delivery service. They too would be delivered tomorrow.

He created his project plan. He'd try to insert turkey DNA into the cucumber genome and then infect it with the zombie turkey virus. That'd double the growth rate of cucumbers easily!

The turkeys, bacteria, and corn arrived the next morning. First, he ensured the zombie bacteria worked. He injected the bacteria into the two birds and watched their eyes turn red. That was the first sign of zombiism.

He had already moved them from standard chicken-wire pens to the Zombie Turkey Farmers of America (ZTFA) approved steel cages. They couldn't defeat the quarter-inch steel bars, but they kept trying. They'd peck at them until they were bloody. Then they'd pause and heal and try again. So that was what Dr. Galloway meant when he wrote that the zombie bacteria caused increased aggression.

Using the Vegan Inc. lab's waldo, he extracted fresh blood from the turkeys and separated out fresh E. coli Gallopavo bacteria. The turkeys pecked at the mechanical hands to no avail. He injected the ECG into living cucumbers at various stages of growth. No effect.

No surprise. Now for the second branch of his research. Even though a cucumber's DNA was far simpler than a human's, he had thousands of sites where he might splice it in. He picked the ten likeliest and planted twenty chimera seeds.

Only half even sprouted. He tested them with the ECG bacteria. Failure. He tried ten different DNA sites each day to make his "turkeycumber," as he called the chimera. After a month of failure, he gave up. He had to try something else.

Scanning the internet for inspiration, Brice read the *Midley Beacon* again. The headline "Zombie Squirrel Caught on Video" leapt out at him.

He read, "The hawk nabbed the squirrel, as hawks normally do, but in midair, the squirrel revived, ripped open the hawk's belly, bit off its leg, and fell a hundred feet to the ground, where it scampered away unharmed. It was captured on drone video."

That's it! He'd try some other animals and see if they'd turn zombie. First, he made a squirrelcumber. No effect. Then a cowcumber. Failure. Then a deercumber. Nothing. Another month down the drain.

His boss, Wilma O'Reilly, stopped by. "Hi, Brice. How's it going?" That meant, "Did you double the cucumber growth rate yet?"

"Success is just around the corner," he lied. He knew what to say to get her off his back.

"That's great! So you'll have this solved in another month?"

That meant she didn't believe his lie.

"Maybe a month and a half. Or two." He had no clue when he'd solve it.

"Fantastic! That's a commitment to have something by June then, right?"

"Uh, right." She had him nailed to a wall. He had three months to solve this, and he was no closer than when he started.

"Wonderful. When you succeed, you'll easily pay for the money you've spent on the research. Oh, and by the way, if you can't solve this problem, we'll have to let you go in the midyear budget cuts. But I'm sure you'll solve it." She smiled brightly and walked away.

Ugh. Now what? His mind was blank. He filled it up with social media. A tweet on a hummingbird picture led him to an article about them. Fastest metabolism of all animals. Insectivores as well as herbivores. Huh. They were like turkeys. They were like turkeys on speed!

Why not? Brice thought. *What have I got to lose—besides my job?* Could he buy hummingbirds on Amazon? Nope. Not legal, since they're migratory birds. But he could become a hummingbird rehabber. He already had a biology degree, as well as a master's in recombinant DNA.

Brice volunteered at the nearest bird rehab center. They were delighted to have him. He nursed several birds back to health, bound broken legs and wings. He also extracted some hummingbird blood and sequenced its genome.

He brought one hummingbird back to the lab instead of releasing it to the wild. He fed it Corn-All GMO grain and studied its droppings for any E. coli. Yes! It produced the zombie bacteria too, just like turkeys.

He sprayed the zombie E. coli (ZEC) at the bird. Soon its eyes turned red. It rammed the birdcage, faster and faster, bending the bars. It was a zombie.

Brice extracted its blood and put it in a cage of bulletproof glass. It settled down, slurping up the nectar from the feeder, eating twice as much as usual. Higher metabolism was another sign of zombiism.

No time to waste. He had only one week left until June. Over the next two days, he spliced the zombie hummingbird DNA into the three hundred spots on the cucumbers' DNA and planted them all.

Only one came up. He injected the hummingbird's zombie bacteria into it. It began to grow even as he watched it, flowering. He hand pollinated it, and by the time he left for home, he had twelve full-grown cucumbers. Success! Brice could hardly wait for the next day.

The cucumber plant filled the lab when he arrived, covered with flowers. He pollinated hundreds of them. Then Brice pickled his twelve cucumbers. Now they just had to pass the taste test. It'd be a week before they were ready.

Brice took the brine solution and sprayed his zombie hummingbird with it. As everyone knew five months after the zombie turkey apocalypse, salt water was the most effective way of eliminating zombiism. He watched the bird until its red eyes turned to black. Then he let it go back to the wild.

"Thanks, little guy," he murmured.

While he waited for the pickling to complete, he picked hundreds of cucumbers. He tested their seeds to ensure the hummingcumber chimera bred true. It did. The second generation grew just as fast. The rest of them he canned in brine.

The next Monday, Brice tasted the pickles. They were a beautiful light green on the inside. They tasted heavenly, better than any pickle he'd ever tasted before.

Brice called Wilma into the lab.

"Hi, Wilma. These are the results of my research."

"Wow! What do you have, a hundred quarts of pickles? How long did that take?"

"That's a week's growth, from one cucumber plant. I've got a couple more plants growing, but we need to transplant them to a field. We'll have to harvest them daily."

"How? I've never seen anything like this!"

"I made one difficult genetic modification. I made a chimera, combining a cucumber with a hummingbird. I then infected it with the zombie bacteria."

"That's insane! What made you try that?"

"I wanted the cucumbers to grow as fast as the zombies do."

"Brilliant. You're promoted to senior researcher right now."

Brice proudly watched the fields of zombie cucumbers grow and be harvested daily all that summer. If left unharvested for a day, the cucumbers turned iridescent green, like a ruby-throated hummingbird. These colorful vegetables became even more popular than the plain zombie hummingbird pickles.

One morning, overlooking a beautiful field of jewel-like green, Brice noticed a waving motion. Walking into the field, he saw the cucumber wriggling on the ground. The wriggling became waving and then flapping. Each cucumber grew a pair of flapping iridescent emerald wings.

In one motion, the entire field of cucumbers rose in a sparkling green murmuration from the ground. With his mouth agape, Brice watched the glittering vegetable cloud head south.

After it was out of sight, Brice looked around the bedraggled field. Not one opalescent pickle remained.

"Hi, Wilma, I've got some bad news," he said into his phone.

"What's that, Brice?"

"The pickles have migrated south."

"What? I have a connection problem. I thought you said, 'The pickles have migrated south.'"

"Yes, that's right. Apparently, the hummingbird DNA is more powerful than I thought. Their migration instinct has been spliced into the pickles."

"You realize that field is worth over a million dollars. You've *got* to get it back."

"Calm down. I have a plan."

"What's that?"

"The pickle hummingbirds will probably instinctively migrate to Mexico, like regular hummingbirds."

"Get going then. We need you to capture those flying pickles!"

"I'm leaving today."

Brice arrived in Mexico City that night. He read the news and tracked the pickles by the news reports and Instagram photos and Twitter gifs. Louisiana. Texas. Reynosa Mexico. Xalapa. Where was that? The picture from Twitter showed iridescent pickles with wings nesting by the thousands in the trees.

He found Xalapa on the eastern side of the Mexican Rockies. He rented a truck, loaded it with the supplies he had shipped with him, and headed there.

Brice drove to the grove where the zombie cucumbers nested. He started the power washer in the back of his truck and headed to the trees, dragging his hose. He sprayed a jet of salt water over the cucumbers, killing their zombie bacteria. They dropped to the ground by the tens of thousands.

Brice then hired local farmworkers to place them in jars filled with brine. He had enough for a whole semi. He didn't catch all the escaped cucumbers, but he had enough to make up for the lost harvest.

After that, Vegan Inc. prevented the pickles from developing to the winged stage. But enough escaped Brice that they became part of the annual pickle migration from Mexico to the US. People captured thousands each year along the Mississippi migration route. Some people felt the wild zombie pickles tasted better than the domestic farm-raised ones. Vegan Inc. took advantage of this and built canning factories in Mexico near the pickle nesting sites.

Vegan Inc. even sold their iridescent wings separately as a pickled delicacy. This became their most profitable item. Until they dried the wings and sold them as earrings.

This story is set just after my first book, Zombie Turkeys. I got the idea for flying pickles while joking with my daughter Tori. When I picked her up to take her somewhere, I'd say, "Watch out for the flying pickles as you go into the car. It's the season for their annual migration." From that, we built up a whole life cycle for flying pickles. Naturally, it had to be in my short story collection.

The Butterfly Effect

by Andy Zach

"Whatcha doing, Brice?" asked my boss Wilma O'Reilly after sneaking up behind me.

I jumped. As usual, I was cruising the internet, bored with my job. How awkward.

We worked at Vegan Inc., an agricultural conglomerate. I was their lead geneticist in charge of enhancing the qualities of the corporation's vegetable products through genetic modification.

Thinking fast, I said, "Uh, researching. I'm reading about the 'Butterfly Effect.' It shows how small changes lead to great changes far away. Like a butterfly's wing causes a cyclone on the other side of the earth." That should work since that was what I was reading.

"How is this related to your current assignment of increasing the yield of our zucchini varieties?"

"I'm trying to relate my past success with cucumbers to zucchinis."

"I'd think you'd just do what you did last time when I promoted you."

"Well, I did, and it didn't work for zucchinis. I tried zombie hummingbird DNA, zombie turkey DNA, and twenty other zombie animals as well. But nothing worked. So I'm stretching my mind to the farthest reaches of what might be possible."

"That might work. Try this scenario for a possibility: if you don't make progress in another month, you'll lose your position. You got promoted for great success. You'll get demoted for failure." Then she smiled sunnily and said "Have a nice day!" as she left.

Great. I couldn't coast anymore. Why did work have to be so much work? And I *had* worked hard, testing twenty species of zombie animals trying to make chimeras with zucchini. There were 173 DNA spots on the zucchini DNA where I could insert the animal or bird genetic sequence.

Those were all the known zombie species, except for humans. Vegan Inc. had strict rules about not editing human DNA. My choices were to create a new species of zombie or do something else to increase our zucchini production.

I didn't know what else to do. My one GMO success had been creating a chimera, a cross between a zombie hummingbird and a cucumber. The zombie hummingbird's super-high metabolism crossed into the cucumber, and they matured to full growth in a week.

Only animals could get zombiism through the zombie bacteria, itself a mutation from genetically modified E. coli bacteria.

People had tried inducing zombiism in other mammals and birds with no success. They had to have E. coli gut bacteria, but out of hundreds of species tried, only twenty worked.

Think outside the box, Brice Butterworth. That was the one thing I was good at. Bird species—check. Animal species—check. Reptiles? They hadn't been tried for zombiism. But they had slower metabolisms. Not a good trait when I wanted faster growth. What else? Insects? They certainly had fast metabolisms. None had shown any zombiism. Perhaps I could induce it. This might give me recognition even outside Vegan Inc. I might even win a Nobel Prize!

Let's see: What insects have a fast metabolism? Flies, fleas, gnats, ants, dragonflies, butterflies, bees, beetles. Praying mantises? Why not? What could go wrong?

Uh-oh. Did any of these insects have E. coli? They needed to host E. coli to become zombies.

After a couple of hours of research, I discovered insects had gut bacteria, but none of it was E. coli. Maybe I could induce zombiism anyway. I didn't really have a choice.

Okay, I needed insect gut bacteria. Could I buy it online? Amazon? Nothing. Google? Zilch. *Looks like I'll have to make my own. First, I've got to figure out how.*

Another four hours of internet cruising taught me

cockroaches, butterfly larvae, and termites were my best bets to zombify. They had symbiotic gut bacteria like human E. coli. That was good. I'd rather have three species than three hundred. I think I only had time to try three anyway.

I could order cockroaches, butterfly larvae, and termites online, so I ordered plenty, with next-day shipping. After all, it was Vegan Inc.'s dime.

I studied the habitats I needed for my creepy-crawlies. I'd use my hummingcumber chimera plants to feed the butterfly larvae. They grew so fast that one plant could feed hundreds of caterpillars. I needed rotting wood for termites. There was plenty in the park near my house. I just needed garbage for the cockroaches. I'd just clean out my refrigerator.

Therefore I had to leave work and go home to clean out my fridge. That was a new reason to take off early!

I never enjoyed cleaning out of my fridge as much as I did that afternoon, knowing my company would pay to me do it. It was a dirty, thankless job, but I was glad to do it in the cause of science.

I put the moldy yogurt and green slices of meat in a plastic pail, along with soft apples and mushy oranges. I added limp celery for bulk and took it to work the next day.

Three packages awaited me on my desk the next morning. Cockroaches to go, termites in transit, and leaping Lepidoptera larvae—caterpillars. I loved the internet!

I dumped the cockroaches into the garbage pail, the termites onto the rotten wood, and the caterpillars onto the hummingcumbers. I sealed each environment in a glass case in my lab. I selected one individual of each insect to sequence the DNA of its gut bacteria.

A week later I had the bacteria DNA all sequenced, and I planned to add in the zombie sequence of E. coli Gallopavo, the zombie turkey bacteria. I double-checked all the enclosures to make sure they were insect and caterpillar proof. The termites and cockroaches were busy reproducing. The caterpillars had tripled in size since I dumped them on the cucumber plants. But nothing escaped the sealed glass containers.

I added the zombie bit to each strain of gut bacteria and then bred them on agar in petri dishes. The bacteria colonies grew and covered the three dishes. Then I contaminated each environment with the new bacteria.

How would I know if it took and the insects became zombies? I'd have to take samples. Starting the next day, I sampled each species and checked the gut bacteria. Zero for three the first day. I reinfected the environments with my still-growing cultures. I also force-fed some individuals the bacteria. I highlighted them with an orange marker.

The following day I checked these individuals. Termite: no zombie bacteria. Cockroach: nothing. Caterpillar: Yes!

I checked three other caterpillars. Zilch. Apparently it wasn't contagious. So I tediously force-fed a hundred caterpillars the zombie bacteria.

I had already planned where I would put the insect DNA into the zucchini. I took my little zombie caterpillar and tried to make a chimera at seven different spots in the zucchini DNA sequence. Seven seeds were planted, each in its own container.

Six of the plants lived and grew. I carefully measured the growth rates. Five were normal, and one was 50 percent faster. This might be my next success. As a backup, I created five more caterpillar chimeras matching that modification. They also grew faster.

I waited impatiently for the plants to flower. The normal time for a zucchini to flower was forty days. My deadline was just two weeks away. Even looking at 50 percent growth improvement, it'd take over three weeks. Could I get an extension from Wilma?

"Hi, Wilma," I said as I called her on my phone.

"Hi, Brice. What's up?"

"I've got the zucchini growing 50 percent faster."

"That's great! I knew you could do it."

"It'll be ripe in three weeks."

"That's fine. I'll drop by for a taste. See ya later. I've got a meeting."

Whew. That was easy. Now I had to make sure nothing went wrong.

I carefully fertilized the seven plants and hand pollinated the flowers. The butterfly zucchini chimera rewarded me with a bumper crop. What should I call it? A zucchinifly? A butterchini? I decided upon zucchinifly. "Zombie zucchinifly" rolled off the tongue.

Wilma showed up a day before the deadline.

"Hi, Wilma. I expected you tomorrow, not today."

"I wanted to see your progress. Wow! These zucchini look great! This is from seed in three weeks?"

"That's right."

"Let me try one."

"Uh, okay." I was nervous. I hadn't tried one yet myself. "I'll have my first one with you."

I grabbed the biggest zucchini and cut it into slices. We each took a bite.

"Gah!" Wilma spit it out on the floor.

"Yuck," I said after gagging out mine.

"That's so bitter. It's like chewing steel wool."

"Or aspirin."

"See if you can find out why it tastes so bad, and get rid of the taste."

"Will do."

A chemical analysis revealed extremely high concentrations of iron, with traces of lead as well. Examining the genetically engineered symbiotic bacteria, I discovered they extracted metals from the soil and concentrated them in the fruit.

I checked the caterpillars too. Some had woven pupae. The concentrations of iron and lead were even higher in them.

"I wonder if these concentrations are too high for the butterflies to live?" I murmured to myself. "It'll be interesting to see if they live."

I planted some zucchinifly seeds in a special hydroponic garden, free of any nutrients except those I added. Maybe I could keep the metals out.

My new plantings grew slowly, even slower than normal zucchini. Meanwhile, the pupae popped into butterflies. Rather than the plain white cabbage butterflies I used, they were white and red—their wing veins were red.

I tested them. They still had the mutant zombie gene. I'd made a new zombie species! The wing veins had all the iron concentrated in them. I wondered what behavioral changes I'd see.

The just-pollinated plants grew larger and larger. Soon they were the size of dinner plates. Meanwhile, my iron-starved zucchini were just flowering. A week later I had zucchini.

I tasted them. Okay, nothing to write home about. So I'd

gotten rid of the bitter taste and fast growth.

"Wilma, I've got good news and bad news," I told her as she walked into the lab.

"Give me the bad news first. I don't want to get my hopes up."

"The bad news is the non-bitter-tasting zucchini I've made don't grow any faster than normal."

"Ugh. What's the good news?"

"They're not bitter."

"That's a bitter pill to swallow. You've spent six months of your time of this project with nothing to show for it."

"It seems without iron or other metals, the fast-growing zombie effect isn't there. The symbiotic bacteria are still there, but they're in a dormant state."

"Hmmm. What will happen if you add iron now, to the mature plants?"

"I don't know. I'll try it."

"I'll try to think of some use for this weird zucchini."

"I've named it a 'zucchinifly' because it's a chimera."

"Woah!" Wendy looked at the huge butterflies ponderously pollinating my cucumber and zucchini plants in the lab. "Are those zombie butterflies?"

"Yup. It's a new species, the first human-made zombie."

"That's something. Congratulations. Write up the paper and submit it for peer review. Keep puttering around with these plants and butterflies and see what you find out."

So now I had my regular job and I had to write a paper that'd pass peer review. I'd have to dig out my old college papers and copy that format.

I experimented adding different metals to the soil. Iron first. How much would the zucchinifly actually absorb? Did it affect the caterpillars? I was now on my second generation of zombie butterflies.

I also tried lead, cadmium, lithium, arsenic, chromium, and mercury. I put biohazard warning signs on my zucchinifly pots. I also put the zucchinifly caterpillars on these plants.

While I waited for the plants and caterpillars to grow, I wrote my paper on the zucchinifly. I documented the DNA modifications in first the cabbage butterfly gut bacteria and then in the zucchini itself.

If anything, the zucchini and the caterpillars grew faster

with the poisonous metal additives. I tested the fruit, stems, and leaves. All the metals were concentrated in the zucchini fruit.

When the butterflies emerged, they were spectacular, with silvery veins of chromium, cadmium, and lithium. The mercury came out as rust-red and cinnabar mercuric-oxide stripes on the wings.

"Those are lovely!" Wilma exclaimed. "We can definitely market those butterflies as art objects. Also, I have a government customer who's interested in using our GMO vegetation to clean up toxic waste sites. You ready to take your zombie zucchiniflies on the road?"

"You bet!"

I began my tour of the US Superfund sites, where the government funds the cleanup of hazardous waste. I felt like Johnny Appleseed planting my zucchinis everywhere across the US. I covered each site's poisonous soil with zucchini plants and zucchinifly caterpillars. After ten or twenty sites, I returned and called in rental zucchini harvest machines and Vegan Inc. trucks.

"Hey, Wilma," I said on my phone as I watched the first harvest.

"Hi, Brice. What's up?"

"What are we going to do with all these zucchini? You know they're poisonous with toxic metals."

"We've got a twofer going! The government is paying us to extract the metals, and then we're selling them to high-tech companies who need them to manufacture integrated circuits. You've come through again, Brice."

"What about the zucchiniflies? I see you've got hundreds of people leaping around the field capturing them."

"That's another income stream. I've hired a thousand lepidopterists to follow the harvest trucks and catch them. I pay them piecework wages, a hundred dollars per zucchinifly."

"Heck, I'll catch them for that rate!"

"No, I need you at the next twenty superfund sites. I'm paying you a per diem for all your expenses, so that's like a raise."

"Thanks, I guess. How do we make money on butterflies when they cost a hundred bucks each?"

"We sell them as jewelry under the brand Iron Butterfly at

nine hundred percent profit. But that's not all."

"What else are you selling?"

"The zucchinis themselves."

"They're poisonous!"

"No, not the iron-enhanced ones. We sell them as iron supplements to the health food market. 'All organic, iron-enhanced zucchinis.'"

"What about the terrible bitter taste?"

"That's become a marketing feature. Our CEO ate one on YouTube and challenged the CEO of our rival Corn-All to eat one for ten thousand dollars, donated to charity. It's gone viral on social media."

"Fantastic. What charity, by the way?"

"The Lepidopterist Society."

I had so much fun with Brice Butterworth I had to write another story. My major challenge was to make it interesting yet different from "In a Pickle." Did I succeed? Let me know.

With the next series of stories we get into the world of *My Undead Mother-in-law*, where humans become zombies—with humorous results.

Zombie Shift

by Andy Zach

He woke up staring out his windshield at the green grass of the highway median. Dully, Anthony listened to the sound of his car's engine cooling, ticking like a clock. He didn't know why he was here or how he got here.

"Hey, are you okay in there?" came a voice from outside the car.

Turning his head toward the sound, he realized he was upside down, supported by his seat belt and his legs, which were strangely numb.

"Uh," he croaked.

A highway patrolman squatted and peered through the passenger window, now broken. "Here. Let me help you." The officer went around his car and opened the driver's door. It scraped the turf, leaving an earthy smell.

He fumbled with his seat belt. With his weight on it, he could barely pop it off. He braced himself with his left hand against the ceiling, removed the weight, and slid it off. Slowly he eased himself down until he was lying on the ceiling with his head out the door on the grass.

"Ow," he said as he wriggled his legs out of the pincer grip of the lower dash and his seat. Odd. He didn't remember scooting the seat so far forward. For some reason, there was only an inch between the seat and the dash.

"Ow. That hurts."

"What hurts? Where do you hurt?"

"My right leg. I think it's broken."

"I've already called the EMT. They'll be here soon." Sirens wailed and then abruptly stopped. "Here they are."

Idly, Anthony watched the flashing lights reflecting off the broken glass of his car.

The EMT personnel braced his neck and back and pulled him out of the car. They put him on the gurney, and the officer walked with them to the ambulance.

"Do you remember anything about how the accident happened?" one EMT asked.

"Uh, no. I was driving home from work—work! Oh no, I'll lose my job over this!"

"Where do you work?"

"The zombie shift, the night shift at the Amazin warehouse, twelve to eight. What'll I do without a job?"

"I'm sure something will work out," said the officer as the ambulance closed.

"We're going to cast your leg," said the nurse in the ambulance. Her name tag read *Louise Tall*, but she didn't seem tall. "What's your name?"

"Uh, Anthony. Anthony Jones."

"Do you know your height and weight, Anthony?"

"Five eleven. Two ten. I need to lose some weight. Ow!"

"Just straightening your leg. We're putting on an inflatable cast. It'll feel better soon. We've given you a local anesthetic for the swelling. What's your medical insurance?"

"Amazin employee healthcare."

Mechanically, Anthony answered her questions. His mind was focused on what he would do if Amazin fired him. It'd taken him years to get hired full time by Amazin, first as a warehouse picker, then as a third-shift lead picker. His family needed his healthcare insurance. His wife was due with their third child in two months.

He still couldn't remember the accident. He remembered leaving work that morning. He'd done twelve hours, starting early and finishing late. They could use the overtime. He'd driven along the freeway the same as always, the sun shining behind him. He went over the hill—and nothing. Just a blank after that.

Now they'd have to replace his work car. He'd bought it used for a thousand dollars, but they didn't have a thousand for a replacement. They didn't even have a hundred.

He supposed his wife could drive him to and from work in her car. But how could he work with a broken leg? He still had less than two years seniority, and they could lay him off at any time for any reason.

After admitting him to the hospital, they brought him his clothing and a bag of his personal items from his car. He called his wife on his phone.

"Hey, Raven, it's Anthony."

"WHERE ARE YOU?"

"I'm in the hospital. I had an accident. I'm okay."

"St. Luke's?"

"Yeah."

"Don't leave. I'm coming." She hung up.

Anthony worried. His wife was eight months pregnant and had their two-year-old and five-year-old, plus her daycare kids to care for. How would she manage?

But she was smarter than he was. He'd never known why she loved him and married him. It was too good to be true. Now, if he lost his job, they might have to move again. Would he lose his wife and kids if he lost his job?

Raven entered his room, rushed to the bed, and hugged and kissed him. Her jet-black hair fell over his eyes.

Abruptly, she straightened. "What happened?"

"I had an accident. I woke up upside down. They took me to the hospital, and I called you."

"How'd it happen?"

"I don't remember. I was just on my way home, climbed the hill on the freeway, drove over the rise...and then nothing."

"You probably fell asleep. You had a twelve-hour shift, and you didn't sleep well yesterday. Are you in much pain?"

"No. They gave me something when they set my leg."

"How long till you can go back to work?"

"That's what I'm worried about. I know three guys at the Amazin warehouse who were fired when they got sick or injured."

"That'd wreck everything we've built here. We'd lose the house, and we'd have to move and start from scratch."

"I know."

Raven's brown eyes looked off into space. He knew that look. She had an idea. He waited for it.

"I have an idea." Raven reached into her purse and brought out what looked like a glue dispenser. The side read *Zom-B Pen—100% zombie blood guaranteed to turn you into a zombie.*

"If you become a zombie, you'll heal from your broken leg and you can go home today."

"Where'd you get that?"

"I bought it with my childcare money. I kept it in case one of us got injured. Becoming a zombie is cheaper than insurance."

That was true. They could barely afford their co-pays. He had no idea how much a stay in a hospital would cost. Zombie blood cured a wide range of injuries and diseases: regenerating limbs from amputations, AIDS, and Alzheimer's. The only side effect was you'd be a zombie with glowing red eyes. People generally looked down on them as weird.

"I don't know..."

"I do." Raven stabbed the Zom-B Pen into his good leg. A sharp stab, then it was over.

"If you don't like it, you can always get the antidote. It's available free at the public health clinic. But at least you'll be past the broken leg."

"How long does it take?"

"Only about twenty minutes to half an hour. What's the car like?"

"Totaled. The roof was crunched. I had to be helped from the car."

"What'd the car cost? Five hundred?"

"A thousand."

"That's still less than the insurance would have cost. Good thing we only got liability. Well, I've got a thousand saved up for emergencies. Go find a new used car. How are you feeling? Better yet?"

"Uh, yeah." He moved his cast and frowned. "No pain at all."

"Let's take off that temporary cast."

"What if it's not healed?"

Raven took out her makeup compact mirror from her purse and stuck it in front of Anthony. "Look."

Anthony saw two red eyes looking back at him. "I don't feel any different. Maybe not as tired."

Raven took off the inflatable cast. "No marks, straight as an arrow, nice and muscular, as usual." She smiled. "Here are your clothes. Let's go."

"Don't we have to check out?"

"I'll tell them the room is free."

On their way home, Raven said, "I'll drive you to work this evening. Can you get a car by the weekend?"

"Yeah. I don't think I can sleep. I've got too much energy."

"Great! I've got a ton of things I want done around the house."

Anthony repaired, painted, and cleaned for eight hours until his wife went to bed. He never slept. But he did eat a steak, a large pizza, a plate of spaghetti and meatballs, and two big hamburgers.

That evening at work, Anthony had no problem keeping up with his normal killer picking schedule. He even had time to help his coworkers. At the end of the shift, he got a "Great job!" from the computer monitor he carried. It showed him where to pick and if he was on schedule. It also tracked how long he took on his bathroom breaks. For the first time, it showed "Attaboy, Anthony!" with a big thumbs-up picture.

When his wife later picked him up and then drove over the hill where he'd crashed, he saw that the car had been towed, with only ruts where it had been. He felt mildly sleepy. Maybe he'd nap when he got home.

* * *

The next night, Anthony noticed his coworker Deandra was crying and asked her why.

"I can't meet my schedule, I'm sick as a dog, and my kids are too! Boss said if I didn't meet my quota again, I'd be fired."

"No problem. I'll help you."

"What's up with you, Anthony? You're working like a house afire! And why are your eyes red all the time?"

"I got the zombie blood treatment after my car accident the other day. I have a lot more pep."

"I'll say! I could use some of that."

"Here. Take mine." Anthony pulled the Zom-B Pen out of his pocket and gave it to Deandra. "Just stab it in your leg, and twenty minutes later you've got red glowing eyes and endless energy."

Deandra took the Zom-B Pen and handed him her computer tracker. "Here, take this. I've got to go to the ladies' room.

Raven had insisted he carry the Zom-B Pen at all times. He could always buy another on his way home.

Anthony finished Deandra's assignment and his and met her coming out of the restroom. Her eyes shone red. He handed her the tracking device.

"Wow! I feel like a million bucks. Thanks, Anthony. Where'd you get that Zom-B Pen?"

"At Farm and Fleet or the Walmart pharmacy. They have the best prices."

"I'll get some for my kids."

Deandra told Joe. Joe took the treatment too, and he told Phil. Phil became a zombie and told Angel and Jesus, and they told eight of their friends. In a week, the whole Amazin third shift had become a literal zombie shift.

Productivity doubled, which put Amazin warehouse management in a quandary. They had planned to lay off everyone and replace them all with robotic pickers, but the workforce was already meeting and surpassing their most optimistic projections for the new robots. The Amazin warehouse officers met to discuss the situation.

"I'm all in favor of saving ten million from the capital budget by not buying these robots," said warehouse comptroller Gene Symonwicz.

"But what if this zombie crew quits? They're all at the top of their pay scale already. How can we motivate them to stay?" said HR manager Audrey Tiffin.

"We can pay a lot of zombies for ten million," Gene pointed out.

"We'd have to make a new pay class," Audrey said.

"We also need statistical proof they're really better than the robots," said their IT manager, Rhoda Gancarz.

"Here's what we'll do," said warehouse VP Sid Bonham. "We'll get one robot for free from the manufacturer. Tell them we're testing it out. We'll test each worker against the robot. Any that can't beat it, we will replace. Those who beat it, they go into a higher pay class. If they all beat it, we'll return the robot."

* * *

"We're going to do some testing of the new robot," said

Jason Dunn, the third-shift supervisor. "We'd like to see how it stacks up with you zombie workers."

"Didn't ya get the memo?" Deandra said.

"What?" Jason said.

"'Zombie' is not politically correct anymore. We're 'paranormal persons.'"

"Uh, okay."

"Deandra's just messing with you, Jason," Anthony said. "We don't really care."

"It was worth it," Deandra said. "The look on your face was worth an hour of overtime."

"Okay. I feel better now. I thought I really stepped in it. I could be fired for that."

Jason continued, "Here's how the test will work. You'll get your regular pick list, and the robot will get an equivalent one. Work at your normal 'paranormal person' speed, and we'll see how the robot compares."

He paused. "I'm not supposed to tell you this, but I believe if anyone beats it, you'll get a raise. I'm not sure how much. Don't tell anyone I told you."

"Paranormal promise!" Anthony held his right hand up, fingers spread, with the two middle ones close together. It looked weird, and that was why the zombie shift adopted it as their sign.

"Paranormal promise!" The whole crew repeated in unison, their red eyes shining brightly, hands raised in the paranormal promise.

Anthony went first. For the first hour, the robot, a wheeled three-foot square with two picking arms and a camera on a stalk, followed him about, picking where he did. Anthony always beat it to the item and to the next. Eventually, it fell so far behind him it no longer followed him. Anthony wasn't worried about the outcome of the test.

Deandra went next. She made no effort to hide her extra speed. After she finished, she said, "I beat that metal box's butt."

And so, through the twelve-hour shift, the entire warehouse crew solidly outperformed the poor cybernetic picker.

The following evening, Jason announced, "Congratulations, paranormal pickers! You've all received adollar-and-fifty-cent pay raise per hour." The whole shift cheered.

But Raven wasn't so happy when Anthony told her about the raise.

"Those pikers! You zombie pickers are twice as productive as normal human pickers. They should have doubled your pay."

"We just take what we can get." Anthony tried to calm her. Raven got touchier the closer she got to her due date.

"You don't have to take what they give you. Take what you negotiate."

"What do you mean?"

"Form a union. Threaten to strike."

"Uh, none of us know how to do that. Every time a union tried to organize, Amazin beat them back."

"So what? I've got an MBA, and I'm smarter than any union negotiator. Nothing compares to negotiating with a two-year-old and five-year-old. Zombies have unique talents. You need a special wage scale."

"You're nine months pregnant!"

"Piffle. I have kids easily. I want to try contract negotiations."

"Okay, Raven. What's our first step?"

Raven typed rapidly on her tablet. "We file with the NLRB, National Labor Relations Board. We enlist the other picking shifts in our union. Then we contact the various national unions. See what they offer. We can use them to pressure Amazin. Then we contact the media. Then we begin negotiations with Amazin. This'll be fun!"

* * *

The next day while Raven talked with the Teamsters, Anthony talked with the workers from other shifts.

By working two hours over at the beginning and end of his shift, he could take a break and talk with the other workers as they checked in and out.

"Hi, Edna," he said to a second-shift worker as she left. "We're thinking of forming a union of warehouse workers. Is that something you can support?"

"Ewww! Get away from me, zombie man!" She turned away

from him, her nose in the air.

"I'd be interested," said a man behind them.

"Great. I'm Anthony. What's your name?"

"Farley. See if you can get more breaks in the day. I can meet my quota, but I'm fifty-seven, and I need more breaks than they give me."

"Will do, Farley."

Those two workers represented the reactions to Anthony's question. He ended up with twenty supporters from each of the other shifts.

Raven wasn't satisfied when he told her his results.

"That won't do. We need more leverage throughout the whole Amazin warehouse network. Little piecemeal efforts don't work. They just close one plant or shift work from one warehouse to another. I've talked with the major unions, and they're all stuck in the twentieth century with their tactics and approach. I'm going to reach outside the box."

"What's that?"

"I'm using the big cannon. I'm contacting SPEwZ."

"Huh?"

"SPEwZ is the Society Promoting Equality with Zombies. They provide free zombie blood for the indigent who are sick. They also pay zombies for their blood donations, which they pack into the Zom-B Pens for cures. Say, you can donate blood. They'll pay a hundred bucks for a pint of zombie blood."

"Not bad. I'll do it."

"Also, zombies can donate daily, since you regenerate so quickly."

"That's like a five-hundred-a-week raise!"

"Or seven hundred. That's thirty-five thousand a year."

"That doubles our income!"

"Yup. They're a pro-zombie organization run by zombies."

"How can they help us with Amazin?"

"They have an enormous network of zombie donors, millions around the world. I'll ask them if any want to help us fight Amazin."

"That'd be amazing!"

Later that day, when Anthony was taking his zombie nap, Raven called the SPEwZ hotline, 1-800-I-ZOMBIE.

"Hi! SPEwZ Inc. Diane Newby here."

"Hi, I'm Raven Jones. I've got an unusual request for

SPEwZ. I'm trying to organize a zombie workers union for the Amazin warehouses. We have some participation, but not enough to win. Can you send my request for support to all your zombie network?"

"Of course! We normally just email them when we have a critical need for zombie blood, and they always come through with thousands of gallons. I'm sure they'll help you."

"I'll send my email request to SPEwZ."

"I don't want that lost in our general corporate email inbox. Send it directly to my personal email: Undeadmotherinlaw@yahoo.com."

"Okay. Let me type that in...it's on the way."

"Just a second as I get it. There it is. Now I'll forward it with my recommendation. How's this sound:

"'Dear Zombie Blood Givers,

"'We don't have a blood need, but our fellow zombies working at Amazin need your help. They're trying to unionize, and they've only found a few zombies to support them. Can you help in any way? I'll do what I can. SPEwZ will boycott Amazin's online store until they allow a union. Very sincerely, Diane Newby.'"

"Wow! That's amazing! Now I sound like my husband."

Diane laughed. "Yes, they do rub off on you after a while. George and I have been married for twenty-five years. How about you?"

"Just six. But they've been the best years of my life."

"Oh! I've got another call. I've got to let you go. Bye!"

"Bye."

Raven received hundreds and thousands of supportive emails from zombies, both within and outside of Amazin. Those within were mostly other warehouse workers around the world in the far-flung warehouse network. So many came in, Raven set up a Mailchimp account so she could mass email them.

Raven created another account for those outside the company. There were even more of these.

Anthony awoke. "Hi, honey. What do you have to eat?"

"I've got a pound of ground hamburger thawing on the counter. Start the grill, and we can have hamburgers. The kids'll like that too."

"Great. How's it going getting support from SPEwZ?"

"Amazin', if I can steal your company's slogan." She glanced at her computer screen, then clicked to the next. "We've got over nine thousand supporters within Amazin, all willing to join our zombie union."

"Amazin'! Can we form our union with that many?"

"Maybe. They're pretty scattered around the world, and that's only one percent of the Amazin workforce. I wouldn't bet on it. But at the rate they're coming in, we'll have ten to twenty times that many in a day. Then I'd be willing to start negotiations."

"This is like a wild story, the kind you like to read." Anthony wasn't much of a reader.

"It gets better. We have about a hundred thousand supporters from *outside* the company. One of them formed a Go Fund Me for us, and we already have ten thousand dollars in it!" She flicked her tablet and said, "Oops. Make that twenty-five thousand."

"We're rich!"

"Uh, no Anthony. This money goes solely the ZEUofA."

"What's zeyu-of-a? It sounds Chinese."

"The Zombie Employees Union of Amazin. I thought the union needed a distinct name from all other unions."

"How will you spend all that money?"

"It's not much at all. I'll hire a corporate labor negotiation lawyer, and this'll last maybe five days. Amazin will spend millions to defeat us."

They talked until Anthony left for work that evening. He'd bought a ten-year-old Taurus for eight hundred. After a couple hundred to replace the brakes, it ran well. They had thirty thousand supporters inside Amazin and five hundred thousand outside. Raven also told him they had half a million in their "war chest," as she called it.

"It's not that much compared to big unions. We could support our thirty thousand members for maybe a ten-day strike."

"Don't worry, Raven. I've got a good feeling about this. I can hardly wait to hear where we'll be when I come back in the morning."

The next morning, Raven waddled out to greet Anthony, her ninth-month belly preceding her. "Anthony! We're all set!"

"Set for what?" He hugged around her stomach and kissed

her.

Gasping, Raven came up for air. "You goof! You asked me a question and then smothered me!"

"No taking it back."

"We're set to start negotiations. That begins with a news release and a television interview."

"How will you get on television?"

"Lisa Kambacher, editor and founder of the *Midley Beacon*, promised exclusive coverage of our union for free. They cover all things related to zombies."

"Yeah, I think I remember them during the zombie turkey apocalypse."

"And also when Diane Newby, the undead mother-in-law, started SPEwZ. Anyway, the media announcement is the start. Then we've got to hold elections and start negotiations with Amazin."

* * *

"Hi. This is Sam Melvin, with the *Midley Beacon*. I have Raven Jones, the founder and leader of the ZEUofA, the Zombie Employees Union of Amazin. Raven, you just won representation of Amazin employees through the NLRB elections. How's it feel to be the first union at Amazin?"

"Amazing—ooo!" Raven clasped both hands over her baby bump and grimaced.

"Are you okay? Should I call 911?"

"Ah, I'm okay. That's just a Braxton Hicks contraction. This is my third pregnancy, and it's no big deal."

"Whew! I'm glad."

"To your question, I'm elated we won, but not surprised. We had the support of sixty thousand zombie employees, and a hundred thousand non-zombies pledged to support us. That's over twenty percent of their workforce. Amazin's scare tactics only persuaded about fifteen percent to vote against us. The real task lies ahead: negotiating a good contract."

"Are you asking for a big pay increase?"

"You'd think so because the zombies are twice as productive as the non-zombie workers, but the bigger needs are job and shift stability and employee benefits. That's what the non-zombies want even more than wages. It'll be tough to get anything from Amazin."

"Will you strike?"

"We will if we have to. I'll ask ZEUofA to authorize the strike, but I prefer not to do that. Amazin has already beaten off many strikes from unions in Europe."

"How can you win?"

"I'm hoping for a groundswell of public opinion against Amazin to sway their corporate board. We've got millions of supporters within and without the zombie community."

"Thank you for your time, Raven Jones. We'll have this livestreamed interview up on our *Midley Beacon* YouTube channel today, for all of you who missed it."

* * *

The first day of contract negotiations with Amazin came. Raven dressed in her navy maternity suit she'd purchased for the occasion. Anthony hovered over her.

"Honey, isn't it close to the due date?"

"Two days past, actually. But those are often wrong by two weeks. I think I've got another week to—oh!"

"Was that another contraction?"

"Of course it was, you dummy! What'd you think it was, gas?" Raven paused and then said, "Sorry, Anthony. I didn't mean to snap at you. I'm just a little on edge."

"It's okay. What with the negotiations and baby David on the way, you've been calmer than you were for the first two babies."

"Are you saying I was snappish?" she snapped.

"Uh, yes, er, no...uh..."

"If you were saying that, you're right. But don't worry. I'll save all my 'snap' for negotiations today."

* * *

"You sure you don't want to use the wheelchair?" asked her Amazin corporate escort, Lucinda Mallory, while she held the wheelchair out for her.

"Nah. This is my third pregnancy. I walked into the delivery room for the first two. It makes for an easier delivery if you stay upright."

Lucinda guided Raven and her lawyer and publicist to the

executive elevator, which whisked them to the top story of the block-sized building.

Several union officials had urged her to negotiate in a neutral site so she'd have more leverage, but Raven preferred to let Amazin think they had the upper hand, that she was a novice and would take the first good offer. No one knew how much leverage she had, not even Anthony.

Walking slowly into the conference room, Raven hid her shock at the twelve unsmiling executives, including Amazin CEO Jafar Zobes, arrayed against her small team on the other side of the table.

The multibillionaire didn't hide his shock. "Is this your whole negotiating team?"

"Yes. Me, Raven Jones; Tiffany Neil, my publicist; and Charles DuCheyne, my lawyer."

"O...kay," Zobes drawled, clearly skeptical. "I will not be involved in the negotiations, but I wanted to greet you and introduce my team." He introduced his lawyers, HR representative, and negotiating team.

"Also, I wanted to shake your hand, Ms. Jones." Zobes did so. "Congratulations, as the first union to bring us to the negotiating table. I trust we'll come to a swift and mutually satisfactory conclusion."

After he left, the lead negotiator, Harrell Barnes, said, "First, let's agree upon our agenda." He gave Raven a sheet of paper.

"Opening statements, fifteen minutes each," she read. "That seems long. I can tell you what we want in one minute."

"All right," Barnes said. He smiled slightly.

Raven smiled inwardly. *He's thinking he's got me.*

"All we want is advance notification of shift changes, a competitive wage and benefits package, and piecework bonuses for those who exceed their quotas. Oh, and the worker quotas are the same around the world and can only be changed by a new contract."

"Here's our initial offer," Barnes said. He passed a folder to her and her associates.

Raven commented aloud, while her companions read their copies. "Workers start at sixteen dollars per hour. Not bad. Two breaks per shift. That's no change. They need to be at least fifteen minutes, and paid breaks as well. Standard medical coverage, standard vacation package." She flipped the pages rapidly, speed reading and marking the contract with a red marker. "No mention of termination policy. No mention of shift changes. No mention of required overtime. I understand you want to terminate unproductive employees and have flexible working conditions. But we are human, not robots, and we need stability in our jobs and family benefits, including emergencies.

"ZEUofA can't accept this contract as is. It has some good points in it, but our counterproposal is in the red marked notes I've made—oooh!" Raven bent over in her chair, moaning.

"Are you all right?" Harrell asked, sounding concerned.

"Ah. Right as rain." She straightened and looked him in the eye. "How long do you need to examine our counteroffer?"

"No time at all. We will not accept anything but our initial offer."

"I thought it might come to this." She plugged her tablet into the projection system. "Now I will tell you what you face.

"Two hundred thousand of your workers are in our union and have agreed to strike. If we do not get agreement today, we go on strike tomorrow.

"I know you usually shift the burden from one warehouse to another. However, we're worldwide, and we'll shut down all your warehouses." The display showed the worldwide network of Amazin's warehouse, which then flickered from zombie red to black.

"But that's the least of your worries. I have three million supporters outside of Amazin who will boycott your goods and services. The total cost of this strike and boycott action will be a billion dollars a day from your bottom line.

"I also have a signed petition from a hundred and fifty thousand Amazin shareholders who promise to sell shares totaling two hundred million should you not sign with us. I estimate your stock price will drop at least a third.

"Finally, we have a strike fund good for a hundred days. For all six hundred thousand employees, in and out of the union. At full pay. That's two hundred days at half pay. Normally, unions don't give this kind of information, but we're not a normal union. That's a two-hundred-billion-dollar hit. On top of the share drop.

"The total cost of our package is estimated at two billion

over the three years of the contract. You'd be wise to ask for a longer contract term. You can lose a hundred times that much this year.

"I think the economic case for this contract, from a shareholder point of view, is ironclad. My associates are emailing the details to your team now."

Raven's complacent smile was replaced by a twisted gasp, "Oh, that's a bad one!"

"Should I call an ambulance?" Harrell said, worried.

"No." Raven breathed deeply. "I'm fine."

"Let's adjourn for this morning," Harrell said. "We'll want to review your counterproposal. I think you may need to go to the hospital."

"No!" Raven snarled. "This is my third child! I know when a baby's coming." Raven continued in her normal tone. "But a break is good. I have to pee. I'll see you at one."

* * *

When Raven's entourage entered the room, only Harrell and two others were there.

"Where's the rest of your crew?" Raven asked.

"They're not needed. We've decided to accept your offer. I reviewed it with Zobes, and we can live with it. These are my lawyers for witnessing the agreement."

"Let's sign it then!"

As Raven signed the last paper with a flourish, she said, "Uh-oh."

"What?" Harrell asked.

"Quick, Tiffany! Your briefcase!" Raven grabbed the briefcase, dumped it on the floor, and then squatted over it as her water burst.

"*Now* you can call that ambulance. The baby's coming."

Harrell escorted her on the gurney, with the EMT personnel, all the way down to the ambulance. He conversed with Raven in between her violent contractions.

"I was afraid this would happen," Harrell said.

"I was afraid it would happen before we came to an agreement. But I planned to adjourn anyway if the baby interrupted our negotiations."

"I have to say, you impressed me. Your preparations

anticipated what we'd offer and what we were willing to concede. I didn't expect the strong shareholder support you had. We ran the names against our shareholder database, and they all matched. I think that's what tipped it in your favor with CEO Zobes."

"Battle preparation is key. Read Sun Tsu."

"I have."

"I was surprised you caved so quickly. I expected a fight and delaying tactics."

"Certainly Zobes wanted to do that. He was willing to take a one-third stock hit in hopes you'd concede some points. I convinced him otherwise."

"How? I thought he was monumentally stubborn and anti-zombie?"

"I, too, have hidden resources." He smiled for the first time, genuine and warm. Then he popped a contact lens off his right eye and waved goodbye to her as the paramedics wheeled her into the ambulance. His right eye shone bright red above his smile as the ambulance door closed.

"Zombie Shift," meaning "third shift," made this an attractive title for me. Combine it with real zombies and my experiences with warehouses, and all the pieces fell into place.

Assisted Living

by Andy Zach

I need to tell you about my own zombie story. It's about how my parents became zombies.

As soon as the zombie turkeys appeared in Illinois, I started cultures of their zombie turkey bacteria in petri dishes. When other animals, squirrels, rabbits, and cows began turning zombie, I added cultures of their bacteria. I sought the ultimate source of animal revivification. It was my PhD thesis and my life's work.

I've always wanted to revive animals from the dead. It seemed the secret was through the special bacteria for each species. Naturally, when humans became zombies, I cultivated their bacteria too.

That's where this story starts. My parents were in an assisted living home, and I brought them to my house for a family reunion. Like all reunions, the house was filled with sisters, brothers, aunts and uncles, and food. Lots of good Greek food—gyros, moussaka, and of course, lots of ouzo, the Grecian licorice liquor. We also had cold cuts and a sandwich bar for the in-laws who didn't do Greek. The trouble began at the bar.

My father, Giorgos "Gyros" Zacharias, loves Vegemite vegetable spread. He usually ate it on whole-wheat bread. He acquired the taste while traveling in Australia for his import-export business. That was also where he got his nickname, "Gyros."

We had the whole-wheat bread, but somehow my wife and I neglected to stock up on Vegemite.

"Anastasios?" he asked me as he pushed his walker toward

me.

"What, Dad?"

"Where's the Vegemite?"

"Oh, sorry about that. I forgot to get it."

"That's okay. I'll just look around for it."

"I don't think you'll find any."

"You'll be surprised. I'm good at finding things."

I was.

The next time I saw him, he was dancing the sirtaki on the patio while playing the "Zorba's Dance" on his bazouki, a Greek mandolin. He eyes glowed bright red.

"Dad! What happened? You've become a zombie!"

"Zombie? Who cares! I feel great! Dance with me, Anastasios. Opa!"

So Dad and Mom and I and the whole family joined in the wild dancing that often accompanied our family reunions. Dad had given Mom a bite of his sandwich, and she threw away her quad cane and danced with us, red eyed.

Afterward, my father said to me, "I thought you said you didn't have any Vegemite?"

"I don't. I forgot to buy it."

"I found some in the basement."

Uh-oh. That was where my lab was. "Show me."

He led me downstairs to my lab, to my table of petri dishes.

"Here's where I found it. There's not much left after I made sandwiches for me and your mother."

He pointed to petri dish forty-two. Just a little dark smear was left of the culture I grew there. I read my notecard below the dish.

"Human zombie bacteria cultured on Corn-All GMO corn."

"I thought it was a little different," Dad said. "It tasted even better than Vegemite! It had a nice corn chip taste."

Other than glowing red eyes, superstrength, and energy, Mom and Dad seemed normal. They insisted that I take them back to their assisted living home. So I did.

That was when things got really weird.

* * *

The next morning Gyros went to his daily shuffleboard game with his friend Sol Blevin at Happy Days Assisted Living

Home.

"Hi, Gyros. What gives with the red eyes? Ya got conjunctivitis?" said Sol, a Korean War veteran.

"Nah, nothing that serious. I just became a zombie."

"Ah. I'd better put on a metal yarmulke to protect my brain."

"That's a myth. Zombies don't eat brains unless that's all we've got. I'd rather have some moussaka. I do get hungry faster. Epatia and I ate all the reunion leftovers for breakfast this morning."

"I'll still beat you at shuffleboard."

"Still? You'd have to have won in the past. I think I beat you yesterday. Anyway, I feel fantastic, and you don't look any better than you usually do."

"I don't feel any better either. Still got arthritis in my legs from my parachuting days. Quit'cher talking and play," Sol said as he picked up his cue.

Gyros picked up his and said, "I'm feeling so good, I'll let you go first."

"You'll regret that," Sol said. He expertly shot his yellow disk down the court, where it rested squarely on the ten-point triangle.

"Hmmph! Lucky," Gyros said.

"Pure skill."

"Watch this." Gyros aimed his black disk at Sol's yellow and shot it as hard as he could. It hit like a bolt of lightning, sending Sol's disk rocketing back, ricocheting upward off the lip of the court and smashing into a second-story window of a bedroom in the wing behind the court. Crashing and yelling sounds came out the window.

"Uh-oh. I guess I'm stronger than I was," Gyros said.

"I just remembered—I've got to go to my colonoscopy exam. See ya, Gyros." Sol hobbled away quicker on his quad cane than Gyros had ever seen.

"Huh. He's never quit a game before."

Meanwhile, Gyros's wife, Epatia, walked briskly to her garden. She was glad to leave her cane at home. That alone made becoming a zombie worth it.

Each resident of Happy Days had a ten-by-ten plot of land. She quickly weeded her garden and then looked at her neighbor's plot. Gertrude Stonemeyer had said Epatia could use it since she was too infirm. It was badly overgrown and had small trees growing in it.

"Let's see how much energy I have as an eighty-eight-year-old zombie," Epatia said to herself. Grabbing her shovel from the shed, she turned the ground as fast as a rototiller. When she hit a tree, she bent over, grabbed it, and pulled it out like a big weed. She went back over the ground, chopping the clods into fine dirt.

Gyros came by. "You did all that?" he exclaimed, looking at the large pile of weeds and trees next to the plot.

"Yes. I'm not even tired. Being a zombie is great for gardening. Now, help me plant my eggplants."

The next morning Gyros met Sol, who looked rather nervous.

"How did your colonoscopy go?"

"Lots of fun. I don't think we should play shuffleboard anymore."

"Why not? You're the only one who gives me a good game."

"But you're a zombie now. It isn't fair."

"Hey, I've been practicing. I've got it under control."

"You know, everyone's afraid of you two."

"Epatia too? She wouldn't hurt a fly. She might make him plant her garden though."

"Anyway, I feel crummy."

"You felt crummy yesterday."

"That was before I found out I had colon cancer."

"Ugh. That's a gut punch."

"You said it. It's stage four. They say chemo could kill me. I'm checking out of Happy Days to go to hospice."

"Say, we just got these Zom-B Pens in the mail yesterday." Gyros pulled a Zom-B Pen from his pocket and read the label to Sol: "Guaranteed to make you into a zombie."

"Why would I want to be a zombie with colon cancer?"

"You don't get it. It's zombie *or* colon cancer. Zombie bacteria destroys all cancers and diseases. It replaces bad cells with good ones."

"Huh. Would it help my arthritis too?"

"Never know till you try."

"Hell's bells, I might as well." Sol took the pen and jabbed it into his leg. "That wasn't any different than my insulin shot."

"We might as well play shuffleboard while we wait for your

zombification."

"Might as well. Losing to you won't make me feel any worse."

But Sol won. Gyros hadn't used his zombie strength, and Sol's pinpoint accuracy was too much for him.

"There you go, Gyros. Even as a zombie, you can't beat me! I feel better already."

"You're also a zombie already."

"If this is what being a zombie feels like, I was an idiot for not getting the shot when it came out."

"Better late than never. Well, see ya tomorrow. Epatia wants me to build a water feature for her gardens."

"That sounds fun. Mind if I tag along?"

"Course not. If we finish before lunch, we can play another game."

After the water feature, shuffleboard, and lunch with Sol, Gyros said to Epatia, "Honey, we need to order another Zom-B Pen."

"Actually two. I gave mine to Delores. She had a mini-stroke yesterday. Let's see." Epatia looked at her tablet. "Hmmm. I get a price break at five and ten pens."

"Get ten. I have a feeling this'll catch on."

* * *

"Hello, Mr. and Mrs. Zacharias. May I come in?"

Gyros looked at the grim-faced Happy Days director, Fred McGan.

"Of course, Fred. What's the problem?"

"Let's sit down first."

Eyeing each other, Epatia and Gyros sat on their couch.

"I heard you and Epatia have been giving zombie blood to the other residents."

"Sure. We offer it to any of our friends with health problems," Gyros said.

"I don't like to do this, but I have to forbid you from doing that anymore. You zombies are scaring our non-zombie residents."

"What a load of horse hockey!" Epatia said. "Why would anyone be afraid of normal, friendly, healthy zombies?"

"It's the red eyes and superstrength. And some believe you

eat brains."

"Crap on a stick!" Gyros said. "Doesn't anybody *read*? That's completely disproven by the thousands of zombies in the US. It was just in the paper the other day."

"I'm sorry, but our board of directors has told me to forbid you from making any more zombies, or they'll kick you out."

"I won't stand for this!" Epatia said, standing up.

"I won't either!" Gyros joined her.

"We'll keep helping our friends, no matter what," Epatia said.

"And if you try to kick us out, you'll *really* have zombie trouble," Gyros said.

* * *

Gyros talked with Sol about the problem over a game of shuffleboard. Gyros had gotten some old fenders from a junkyard and welded them into a barrier around the court. Now they could use their zombie strength, and disks just ricocheted around the court, adding complexity and excitement to the game. As usual, a group of residents watched the game from Adirondack chairs on the deck above them.

"Sol, I'm worried," Gyros said as his shot knocked Sol's disk off the eight-point area, into the back fender, off the side, and directly toward Sol.

Sol deftly caught the ricochet in his left hand, and his right slid the cue into his disk. Streaking down the court, it hit Gyros's disk, blasted it into the side fender, where it bounced back onto the court, wiping out Gyros's two disks in the seven-point areas.

"Hmph. Good shot, Sol."

"You worry too much, Gyros. This zombie kerfuffle will work out."

"We got our eviction notice last night. They're kicking us out for giving zombie blood without a medical license."

"That's no good. Zombie blood is an over-the-counter supplement. The medical community won't touch it with a ten-foot pole. They don't have a legal leg to stand on."

"I know you used to be a lawyer. Do you think you can help us?"

"Nah. The courts move too slowly to resolve this in thirty

days. We'll have to do something else." Sol paused. "Lemme talk with some of my friends. I'll see what I can do."

* * *

Gyros and Epatia packed their apartment. Tomorrow they had to move out. Sol came by with his friend Luther Brockwell. Luther's eyes glowed red under the green eyeshades he always wore. He'd had Alzheimer's until he became a zombie. The zombie bacteria fixed his brain right up as good as new.

"Hi. I have some good news," Sol said.

"What's that?" Gyros said.

"I got a staying order for the eviction notice. It's not just you, but all the other zombies they're trying to evict."

"How many of us are zombies now? Ten or twelve?"

"Nope. We're up to twenty of the forty residents."

"Aren't they cutting their throats by ejecting paying customers?"

"Nah. Happy Days is one of the best senior-care homes. They've got a waiting list a mile long. People are dying to get in."

"So how long is the staying order good for? Should we unpack and stay or move out?"

"It's good until the court hearing next month. We should have some ammunition by then."

"Ammunition? What are you talking about?"

"Luther here used to be a CPA and comptroller. Tell Gyros what you suspect."

"Hanky panky. Once I was back to normal, I started tracking our monthly payments to Happy Days. We're paying a lot for this place, but the Happy Days' annual report shows way more expenses than is reasonable. I've hired external auditors to check their books."

"How can you do that? Don't you have to go to court?"

"No. I was a significant shareholder when this place was built, and then when I got sick, I lost track of its management. Now I'm checking again."

"You should have been there for the board meeting last night," Sol said. "I think the other members needed adult undergarments when Luther told them he'd hired auditors."

"Whoa. When is this audit going to happen?" Gyros asked.

"Right now. The auditors I've hired have frozen all computer access so they can't delete records," Luther said. "They came during the board meeting and locked all the offices. Then they began last night."

"So we don't have to worry about security ejecting me and Epatia?" Gyros said.

"Not when the directors have to worry about being ejected themselves," Luther said.

"When will we find out the results?" Gyros asked.

"At the hearing," Sol said.

* * *

The hearing room was packed. Nearly all the residents had come, most of them zombies. Thirty-five pairs of red eyes watched as the auditors, Slant and Company, presented their report.

"We have examined the Happy Days Assisted Living Home records using usual accounting practices, and here is our conclusion.

"The Happy Days Assisted Living Home is billing their residents twice their expenses. Further, this limited liability company is billing Medicare fully for every resident, falsely claiming every resident is indigent, using fraudulent powers of attorney. They have worked with residents' relatives to get the powers of attorney. They then split the Medicare and Medicaid payments with them.

"We have contacted the district attorney, and he has filed charges against four of the five owners. They have been arrested. The fifth, Mr. Luther Brockwell, has agreed to run the company until new owners can be found."

The judge looked on impassively. "Mr. Brockwell? Will you continue to evict the zombie residents in question?"

"Absolutely not, Your Honor," Luther said as his red eyes glowed into the judge's.

"In light of this information, this whole case is moot. Dismissed. Adjourned." The judge banged his gavel and stood.

The Happy Days' residents peppered Luther with questions as they walked out.

"Who will run Happy Days now?"

"Will Happy Days go bankrupt?"

"Where will the new owners come from?"

"All in good time. We'll have an all-resident meeting when we get back to Happy Days," Luther said.

Back at Happy Days, the residents and most of the employees gathered in the community room. Luther entered with Sol and Gyros.

"Okay, everyone, quiet down!" Gyros bellowed. "The floor's yours, Luther."

Luther stood. "Here's what will happen. First, what will not change. The current employees will continue on, same pay, same benefits. The auditors found no malfeasance with any of you."

The employees and many of the residents cheered.

"Regarding governance of Happy Days, we'll have an elected residents' panel who will work with Happy Days directors to address your needs and concerns."

"Hooray!" "Way to go!" and "Yay!" echoed around the room, along with some whistles. Many of the residents waved their canes in the air. They didn't need them anymore but had brought them to the meeting to wave and get attention.

"Next, we have new ownership. The new owners are our own residents Gyros and Epatia Zacharias and Solomon Blevin. They have pooled their IRAs and bought out the old investors."

The cheers went on long and loud at this.

"The final good news is everyone has a choice of part ownership of Happy Days or reduced monthly cost. This is our dividend for not cheating residents anymore."

Everyone stomped and yelled for many minutes. Then Gyros hollered again, "Quiet, everyone! I have an important announcement."

The crowd paused expectantly.

"I've ordered a Greek meal for everyone, and drinks are on the house. Opa! Let the party begin!" Gyros pulled out his bazouki and began to play and dance.

Both of my parents avoided assisted living, but my mother-in-law is in a facility now. My wife and I have discussed what would happen if all the people in assisted living became zombies (my kind of zombie), and this story came out.

A Dying Business

by Andy Zach

He was dead. At least, his business was. And without his business, his wife would leave him and take their new baby. Then he might as well be dead.

His dad had run the Elysium Fields Mortuary for thirty years and had made a killing at it. The first and only mortuary in their small town of Hillvale, everyone got buried there. He charged normal prices, he was friendly, and he helped their community. His dad said to him when he was a teen, "Irving, after you get your college degree, go to mortuary school, and when you come out, I'll hire you and then turn the business over to you. You'll be set for life."

Irv had no other plans. He liked this cute blonde Shelley in high school, and she liked him. So he learned the business, got his degree in psychological counseling, and came back and married her. Just as he promised, his dad turned Elysium Fields over to him after a few years and retired to Florida with Mom.

The first years had been great. People were dying to be his customers. He and Shelley remodeled his parents' old house, went on vacations around the world, had his and her luxury cars. Shelley had their son, Nathan. Then the bottom dropped out of his business.

Rather than dying normally, people were taking zombie blood. Lung cancer? Gone. Heart disease? Cleared up. Severe accidents? Limbs grew back. Most people then took the vaccine to remove the zombie disease, because who wanted to be a zombie with glowing red eyes? But they were still alive and healthy.

Irv researched the zombie disease during his many idle moments waiting for customers. No one knew how long people with zombiism lived. Zombie turkeys, squirrels, and corgis lived past their normal life span. Humans near death came back as zombies and started living like twenty-year-olds.

All that Irv had left was a trickle of people who died suddenly or who refused the zombie treatment. Irv rejoiced that the prejudice against zombies was so strong, or he'd be bankrupt.

To make matters worse, the zombies had organized themselves. Their leader, Diane Newby, also known as "the undead mother-in-law" started the Society Promoting Equality with Zombies, or SPEwZ. They fought for zombie rights and to make zombies normal and accepted. SPEwZ also collected zombie blood donations and repackaged it in one-dose injectors, Zom-B Pens. These they sold worldwide, making tons of money.

Irv seethed. He called the SPEwZ helpline to give them a piece of his mind, 1-800-ZOMBIES.

"Hello, SPEwZ Inc. How can I help you?" said a pleasant-voiced woman.

"Let me talk to your boss," Irv growled.

"One moment. I'll transfer you to Diane Newby."

Good. He would get right to the top.

"How may I help you, Mr...." came a strong alto voice.

"Isling. Irving Isling. Mrs. Newby, let me give you—"

"Interesting initials," Mrs. Newby interrupted. "Sorry. You were saying?"

"Mrs. Newby—"

"Call me Diane. There's no need to be formal with me."

"I'm the owner of Elysium Fields Mortuary, and your organization is killing me!"

"I'm sorry, but isn't it better to have people alive than dead?"

"Not for me! My father built this business over thirty years ago, and it's about ready to go under—all because of you zombies."

"Hey, we didn't ask to become zombies. We just want to be treated like any other American."

"That's fine, but don't go around selling your zombie blood and keeping people alive unnaturally."

"How bloodthirsty! If you were near death, wouldn't you want a new lease on life?"

"Well, yeah. But still, you're driving me out of business."

"That's the great American way. One business dies, and another rises to take its place. Adapt. Don't be an old fuddy-duddy."

"Fuddy-duddy? I don't even know what that means. I'm only twenty-six."

"It means you're a stick-in-the-mud. Inflexible. Stubborn. Now I'm forty-nine and leading the zombie "craze.""

"I *have* been called stubborn. Mostly by my wife."

"Hop on board the zombie train. We're leaving the station. We can barely meet the demand for zombie blood. There are new zombie businesses popping up daily."

"Like what?"

"Just today, here in SPEwZ headquarters in Gary, Indiana, we put out a job offer for a zombie counselor. People need time to adjust to the new zombie lifestyle and reassurance they're as normal as anyone else."

"Hmmph. How is anyone with glowing red eyes normal?"

"Eyes can always be covered with contact lenses."

"I do have a degree in consoling. Do I just replace my mortuary with a consoling business?"

"Why not both? People will always need to be buried and deal with grief. Even zombies can die."

"So I do have hope. Do I just add a zombie-consoling shingle to my mortuary?"

"Of course. I'll even route zombies we know to you."

"We're pretty sparsely populated here in Hillvale. The town population is just five hundred."

"Let me do a query on our zombie database. Okay, there are one hundred and seventy-five within a radius of twenty miles."

"That's way more than I thought!"

"I can't send you their contact information without violating their privacy, but I can tell them about your consoling business. What will you call it?"

"Um, Elysium Fields Consoling?"

"Got it. I'll send out the email today to everyone within a hundred miles. That's over a thousand zombies."

"Thanks, Diane. I called to read you the riot act, and you

helped me."

"That's what we do here at SPEwZ: help zombies and help people who help zombies."

Irv asked the town printer to make some *Elysium Fields Consoling* signs. He set up a small conference room in their mortuary as an office and mounted a sign on the door, under the foyer sign, and on the outside sign.

The next day he had five emails asking for help adjusting to zombie life. He called each person and scheduled them to come in. One could come that afternoon, a Mrs. Persimmon.

A large luxury car pulled up into his otherwise empty parking lot. A wizened little old lady came out of the huge car, barely able to see over the open door. Then she flipped the door closed with a solid THUNK Irv could hear through the window of his air-conditioned office.

Holding her large black handbag in one hand, her eyes hidden behind huge dark glasses, she skipped—*skipped*—from her car to the front door of Elysium Fields.

Irv closed his mouth and hurried to greet her. The door flew open before he reached it.

"Mrs. Persimmon?"

"Right as rain, sonny." She cackled, looking up at him with a wide grin.

"Pleased to meet you. I'm Irv Isling, director and counselor."

"So you're not a zombie? How will you be able to help me?" She took off her dark glasses and put them in her purse. Her red eyes glowed at Irv with skepticism.

"Um, no, but I do have training in helping people adjust to trauma in their lives."

"Well, being a zombie's a picnic. It's other people that give me grief."

"Come into my office and we can talk about it."

"I don't know about that. Why should I pay you if you don't know what I'm going through?"

"If I can't help you, I'll say so and there'll be no charge."

"Okay then. I can't beat that."

When they were seated, Irv said, "Tell me your story from the beginning. Take as long as you'd like." This was an approach Irv took with grief counseling, getting people to talk about their loved ones.

"When I got my stroke, I couldn't walk or take care of myself anymore. My kids wanted to put me in a nursing home. I thought I'd try this zombie blood thing instead. When my shot came in the mail, I got my home nursing assistant to give it to me. That was the start."

"What happened after that?"

"I popped right out of bed and straightened up the house. I had plenty of energy left, so I mowed the lawn and finished up by playing hopscotch on my driveway. I haven't done that for seventy-eight years. I felt like a young girl again. But that was the start of my problems.

"My neighbors called my kids, and they came over and fussed over me. I was glad they were concerned, and I thanked them. Then we had a fight. They still wanted me to go into a nursing home, and I refused. In fact, I revoked their power of attorney. That really ticked them off. My son tried to drag me off." Mrs. Persimmon chuckled. "That didn't turn out well for him."

"What do you mean?"

"I turned him over my knee and spanked him. I hadn't done that for over sixty years. But now my kids aren't talking to me, and they're threatening legal action. Dumb kids. I've got *way* better lawyers than they do and more money."

"What can I do for you?"

"I'd like to be reconciled to my kids, but they're in a huff and not listening. I don't think they like zombies either. They want me to take the vaccine. There's no way that'll happen. I like roller-skating around my neighborhood like I did as a girl. Did you know these new-fangled inline skates are *lots* better than the clip-ons I had as a kid?"

"No, I didn't. Let me think a minute. You need to meet at a neutral place. Is there a nice restaurant where you can meet as a family and have a meal and discussion?"

"Yes. We can go to Pierre's. We were just there celebrating their thirty-fifth wedding anniversary and my ninetieth birthday, before my stroke. Everyone loves it. I can get a private room again."

"Good. See if you can just tell them what you've told me. Tell them how much you love feeling like a young girl again. Tell them how much you love them and want to spend time with them, not in a nursing home. Don't argue or yell or fight."

"Sonny, you talk sense. I don't know why I didn't think of that. Probably because they stirred up my dander and I wasn't thinking straight. I'll do that. But I want you to come, in case a fight breaks out. Then you can mediate."

"Uh, okay, if it fits my schedule."

"Let's see what we can work out." Mrs. Persimmon reached into her purse and pulled out a golden tablet. She rapidly punched buttons, and then a face appeared.

"Hi Amanda, it's your granny."

"Hi, Grandma. You're looking great!"

"Thanks, honey. Can you and Trevor make it to Pierre's for supper this Friday? It's my treat."

"We'd love to!"

"Great. Now see if you can get your mom and dad to come too. I'd invite them, but they're not talking to me. Tell them it's my treat and there'll be no fighting. I've even hired a counselor to reconcile us."

"I'll try, Grandma, but they're pretty sore at you."

"Tell them I'm dropping my legal action if they stop theirs."

"I'll do the best I can."

"Don't worry, honey. You're the apple of your dad's eye, and he'll do whatever you want."

"Don't I wish!"

"Trust me on this. That's why I called you."

"I will, Grandma."

"Thanks, honey. I've gotta go. Toodles!"

"Bye."

Turning to Irv, Mrs. Persimmon said, "Now I made it for Friday evening. Can you come?"

"Usually I spend Fridays with my wife and son eating out."

"Great! Bring them along."

"My son's only a year and a half. He might be disruptive."

"That's a good disruption. My son William and his wife, Wendy, love kids. We're all very experienced."

"What about Pierre's? I don't know if a luxury restaurant is the right place for an eighteen-month-old baby."

"No problem. We have a private room, and they'll do whatever I say."

"If you're game, then I'm game."

"Good. Now, how much do I owe you?"

"This first session was free, like I told you."

"You've been a big help, and I want to pay you."

"My normal rate is thirty-five dollars an hour, but you don't have to pay, Mrs. Persimmon."

"Nonsense. A man is worth his hire." She told out a thick wallet from her purse and riffled through the bills. "Hmmm. Nothing smaller than a hundred."

"I've got change."

"Don't bother. Keep the change." She handed him a Franklin.

"I feel I ought to pay for my meal now at Pierre's."

"Nah. I eat there every week and get way better discounts than anyone else. It's been nice talking with you, Irv." She bounced up and vigorously shook his hand.

"See you Friday!" she called as she skipped out the door.

* * *

Irv and Shelley left Pierre's late Friday, carrying Nathan in his car seat.

Irv sighed. "Nathan's asleep. That makes the whole evening perfect as far as I'm concerned."

"You and Mrs. Persimmon really seemed to hit it off," Shelley said.

"I just gave her the least amount of guidance, and she ran with it. Her son responded reasonably."

"I think Nathan put everyone in a good mood. Nothing like a cute toddler. And the food was good."

"Wrong. The food was *great*. I can hardly wait for my next counseling session."

"When is that?"

"Monday. Mr. Klikkitat."

"Odd name."

"Yeah. I'll find out what he's like Monday."

* * *

Mr. Klikkitat was middle-aged and pudgy, with glowing red eyes. He sat in Irv's office.

"How can I help you, Mr. Klikkitat?"

He sighed. "Make my family accept me as a zombie."

"Start from the beginning."

"I was morbidly obese, over five hundred pounds. My

doctor said I was sure to die of heart disease. In desperation, I tried zombie blood. In a year and a half, I've lost three hundred pounds. My family's been harassing me to get the vaccine and 'clear up' my red eyes now that my heart is healthy again and I'm at a normal weight."

"How do you feel about getting the vaccine?"

"Terrible. I don't like being pressured into things, and I love how good I've felt as a zombie. Why can't we just get along?"

"That's the question, isn't it? Have you tried contact lenses?"

"Uh, no. My eyesight is fine."

"You can get colored contact lenses to hide your red eyes."

"I'll try that! I won't mention them and let them assume I took the vaccine. Thanks, Mr. Isling!" Mr. Klikkitat rose and vigorously shook Irv's hand.

The other zombie counseling customers also successfully overcame their difficulties. Irv found zombies to be good people with positive attitudes. Although he only had one funeral that week, he covered his expenses and a little bit more. If his counseling business picked up a little more, he'd be back to his old income level.

Sunday night his father called.

"Irv?"

"Hi, Dad. I'm glad to hear from you."

"What's this I hear about you helping zombies?"

"Oh, I just put my counseling degree to use, to fill in idle time between funerals."

"You realize they're our enemy, right?"

"Uh, no, they're just regular people trying to cope with life."

"They're destroying the funeral home business! How much is the business down since they came along?"

"About sixty percent."

"Our gross margin was only fifty percent. No wonder you looked for other sources of income. But you chose badly. I heard from my friends in the National Funeral and Mortuary Association that they're going after you."

"What do you mean?"

"I mean they want you to stop your zombie counseling. They can be very persuasive. They might threaten to kick you out of the NFMA and revoke your license."

"Oh, c'mon, Dad. They're conservative businessmen. They wouldn't be that extreme."

"Because they're conservative businessmen they'll kick you out. They can't have anyone undermining their business. Your business. Our business, that I gave you. Do you want to destroy everything I've given you?"

"No, Dad. I'm just adapting to changing times. Zombies are the new thing, the new medical treatment. They can still die, so they'll come our way eventually."

"I doubt the NFMA will agree. Zombies are killing the mortuary business. I've warned you, Irv. You're an adult and business owner. I wash my hands of this now. Goodbye."

Dad hung up. His own father, Ichabod Isling, founder of Elysium Fields Mortuary, hung up on him.

The next day two burly men in black suits and dark glasses visited him.

"Mr. Irving Isling?" asked the taller one. His hair brushed the doorframe to Irv's office.

"Yes?"

"Is it true you've been counseling zombies in your funeral home?" asked the shorter but wider one. He appeared to be refrigerator-sized.

"I provide counseling services to everyone. I am a licensed counselor as well as a funeral home director."

"Everyone, including zombies?" continued the shorter one. His voice was deep but quiet.

"Yes, and non-zombies too."

"We urge you not to console zombies anymore," said the taller one.

He didn't say "Or else," but Irv heard it in his tone.

"Why not?" Irv felt belligerent. "Who are you anyway?"

"We're your friends," said the brick-wall "friend." "We're trying to protect you from harm."

"What kind of harm? Are you threatening me? Maybe I should call the police."

"You do that," said the door scraper. "We have inside information from the NFMA that they may revoke your license. We're trying to help you."

"Is the NFMA trying to threaten me? I'll fight them in court. I just passed the state inspection. All my fees are paid."

"NFMA recently passed a bylaw that any zombie support

services are unprofessional conduct. They will revoke your license and file charges with the state attorney general."

"Charges? On what grounds?"

"Unprofessional disposal of dead bodies. All zombies are considered dead bodies."

"You play too many video games. Real-life zombies are alive, not dead bodies."

"You have been warned. Goodbye." They turned and left.

* * *

Driving home from work, Irv got a call. Turning on his hands-free speaker, he said, "Irv Isling, Elysium Fields Mortuary."

"Mr. Isling, this is the National Funeral and Mortuary Association."

"What can I do for the NFMA?"

"We regret to inform you that we have revoked your membership and funeral license. We have already done this through the state attorney general."

"You can't! I pay my taxes and my fees. I've done nothing wrong."

"Your unsanitary handling of dead bodies is unacceptable. We have photos and videos of you shaking hands with zombies."

"I'll fight you in the courts!"

"The law is on our side. Unclean working conditions are grounds for license revocation."

"Over my dead body!" Irv swung his car off the busy highway onto a side road so he could park and rant safely. Sadly, he didn't notice the oncoming truck.

* * *

Irv awoke in cold, chilly darkness. The still, stale air had a hint formaldehyde. Where was he? He reached out and touched cold walls, a stone ceiling just above his face, and a hard, metal surface below him. A shelf? No, it was a *drawer.* In horrified certainty, he reached toward the oppressive ceiling and *pushed* toward his feet. Straining, he shoved the heavy mortuary drawer out, from the inside.

Outside, he realized all he wore was a light burial gown,

the kind his mortuary used to cover newly delivered bodies. Turning on the light, he saw it heavily splotched with ochre. Blood. His blood.

He scurried to the bin where his mortuary disposed of the loved ones' clothing. It just contained his suit, torn and clotted with blood.

Aghast, he ran into the bathroom, took off the gown, and examined himself in the mirror. No injuries. No scars. Everything was normal. But his eyes glowed red back at him.

He was a zombie!

He put his burial gown back on and then his suit pants. He opened the heavy mortuary door and immediately heard weeping. The age-old sound of grief eased his beating heart. He wondered whose funeral or visitation was underway, or was a visitor seeking burial advice?

Wait. His home was de-licensed. He wasn't there. What was going on?

He walked into the visitation room and saw his wife weeping with Mrs. Persimmon and Mr. Klikkitat.

"There, there, honey. Get it all out. You'll feel better," Mrs. Persimmon murmured.

"Hi, Shelley. Why are you crying?" Irv said.

"Irv!" she gasped. She stood still, mouth agape.

"What's the matter?"

"You're dead! I saw your poor body after the truck hit you. I laid you in the slab myself. But you're a zombie now. How did that happen?"

Mr. Klikkitat pulled out an injector marked *Zom-B Pen* and said, "I guess these things work."

One of my relatives ran a mortuary for many years, and I also had a friend who ran one. The impact of the zombie phenomenon upon this industry just seemed to write itself.

Red-Eye Fashion

by Andy Zach

The Taser hit me in the back. I convulsed uncontrollably, shocked out of sleep.

"Okay, wakey, wakey. Time to go model for your mistress," squeaked a high tenor.

The bearded hulk who guarded us held his Taser ready, in case Lulu and I weren't fast enough. He was so hairy, I couldn't tell where his beard ended and his chest began. We donned the haute couture apparel set before us. He nodded his approval and gestured toward the door. He always followed us with his Taser.

"We've been here weeks and we don't know your name. What shall we call you?" I ventured. I had some vague hope of putting him at his ease so we could escape.

He laughed. "Call me Gronk." He wheezed when he laughed.

So I got him to laugh. Maybe that was progress. Maybe not. He also laughed when he tortured us with the Taser.

"Let me check you, Sharon," Lulu whispered. She examined my back, where the Taser had hit my sleeping form. My muscles still ached. "No marks."

"Good." We were responsible to keep our bodies perfect, even when tased. If we came to a photo session with marks, then we *really* suffered.

"Contacts," Gronk said.

We each inserted the red-tinted contact lenses that made us look like zombies. Zombie models were the latest craze in fashion. Zombies had an especially high metabolism and quickly acquired a lean, ripped, muscular build. Combined with their exotic glowing red eyes, they'd taken the fashion world by storm.

That was how we got trapped into zombie supermodel slavery. Lulu and I had been zombies for a year already. We were lean and ripped before we voluntarily took zombie blood. We were professional bodyguards for eccentric billionaire Sid Boffin, when his superyacht was conquered by US Marines and zombies.

Sid, as we had suspected, was not merely a megalomaniacal billionaire but also a supervillain. Lulu and I barely survived, thanks to the undead mother-in-law, Diane Newby.

A month ago we were looking for work and running out of money, when Lulu called to me. "Hey, Sharon, look at this ad: 'Zombie Supermodels Wanted.' Top salaries paid for zombie-next-door appeal.'"

"We're certainly zombies. I modeled before I quit to pursue my CrossFit career rather than a starvation diet. Do you think I have zombie-next-door appeal, Lulu?"

"Sure! With your blond hair and blue eyes, you're a stereotypical American."

"Although I'm British. And six feet tall. And forty pounds too muscular to model."

"You're a shoo-in. But not me. I'm too short and dark and Mexican, and I've never modeled."

"You're completely mad, girl. You're absolutely gorgeous. They need Hispanic models. You look as good as Salma Hayek."

"Thanks. But will my MMA career count against me?"

"Don't mention it on your résumé. Just cover your cliff-diving and rock-climbing career in Acapulco. Oh, and add you're a kickboxing instructor."

"That's true. I sure educated my MMA opponents." Lulu laughed.

"We'll go together, and they'll hire us together or nor at all."

"Deal." We shook on it.

The owner of Red-Eye Fashion enthusiastically hired us the next day.

"You're ideal!" Sally Bellows gushed. She was tall, thin, and perfectly dressed with sunglasses that would pay for our food for a month. "Sharon can model for the US, British, and

Scandinavian markets, and Lulu can model for our Hispanic clientele. When can you start?"

"Today," I said. "When do we get paid?"

"We can give you an advance on your salary right after you fill out this paperwork." She handed us each a folder of forms. "Please go to our orientation room." Sally pointed to a red door in the back of the room.

We entered a bare room. No chairs, furniture, or rugs—just a glowing ceiling.

"What's this?"

"Sharon, I've got a bad—" The floor opened under us, and we fell twenty feet into water. Stabbing pain ripped along my right leg and left foot as spikes pierced us.

I started to scream and then tasted the water. "Salt water! Lulu, they're trying to de-zombify us!" Injecting salt water was a quick and painful way to kill the zombie bacteria.

"Quick! Let's get out of here before we lose our strength." Lulu unimpaled herself and broke the spikes with her zombie strength and tore them out of my leg and foot. We went to the wall of the tank and beat it. Solid concrete.

"Boost me up, Sharon." We swam to the bottom. Lulu got on my shoulders, and I kicked off the bottom. I had been an Olympic swimmer, and as a zombie, I was twice as strong. We both cleared the water like a whale breaching. Then I pushed Lulu's feet up with my hands while she kicked. I shot down and she rocketed upward and grasped the lip of the tank.

I fell flat on my back to avoid the spikes, so I had a good view of the blinding spark of the Taser as it hit Lulu. She fell toward me, paralyzed. I caught her and saw a hulk peer over the edge.

"Nighty-night!" he said cheerily as he tased me.

* * *

We awoke, healed but no longer zombies. I quickly checked for my spare zombie blood pens and ampules, but they were gone, as was my clothing. Instead, Lulu and I wore simple nightgowns. We lay on cots in a small, bare dorm room.

The door opened. "Mornin', beauties!" said the hair hulk with a big grin. "Here's the boss. Don't try anything." He pointed his Taser at us.

"Welcome to Red-Eye Fashion," Sally said as she entered carrying hangers of clothing. "You've gotten your first payment—dezombification. We love the zombie look but can't take any chances with zombie models escaping or going to our competitors. You'll wear red zombie contacts for the duration of your stay."

"How long will that be?" Lulu asked.

"As long as we need you. Just remember to do everything we ask. Our guards tase first and ask questions later. Here are your clothes for our first modeling session. If you do well, you'll get fed." She walked out.

We settled into a routine of twice-daily modeling and daily feeding. We discussed escape each night, as long as we could stay awake. Twice we tried to take the Taser from Gronk. I was not as fast and strong as I had been, but I still knew martial arts. He backhanded me and tased me into unconsciousness.

Lulu did better. She clung to the wall above the door before he came in, and dropped on him, wrapping around his neck and choking him. Before I could kick him, he banged Lulu against the doorframe hard enough to knock her out. This time I got a fist in the jaw before being tased.

Since then we'd been careful to be good "zombies" and models. We studied the path to and from our room to the modeling area.

We quickly ruled out an escape from our room. Built with concrete construction, with just a bathroom and cots, a prison cell couldn't be more secure. Our solid-steel door had no handle. It opened electronically from outside.

Other cell doors lined the concrete hall. The bare modeling room contained only props brought in for each modeling session and a green screen behind us to add various CGI backgrounds. Our sole hope was a single door next to the screen. It too was steel with no handle.

"Do you think we can take the Taser from Gronk?" Lulu asked at night as we lay on our cots in the dark.

"We tried and failed."

"How about if we both jump him together?"

"I don't have your climbing skills. I can't hang between the doorjamb and the ceiling."

"How about if you attack when he opens the door and I follow you and catch him off guard? If I get one kick in, I'll break his knee or jaw."

"We can try that. Maybe he's relaxed his guard."

"Tomorrow morning?"

"Why not? Wake me when you get up." Lulu was a light sleeper and always awoke before Gronk entered.

We showered the next morning and took our places beside the door. We made our pillows into rolls under our covers so our beds looked occupied.

The door opened outward. We waited for Gronk's "Wakey, wakey" call. It didn't come

"Wake up!" a deep, strange voice hollered.

Zap! The Taser hit my pillow.

Instantly I attacked. The strange guard was defenseless with his Taser out. I barreled into a lanky, sinewy guy with hollow cheeks. He hit me with a cattle prod in his left hand, while his right held his empty Taser.

Spasming, I fell to the ground. Lulu vaulted over me and kicked at his hand holding the prod. He flicked his wrist, and her barefoot connected with the business end of the prod. Writhing in pain, she fell atop me.

"Bad girls. You have ten seconds to get to your feet, or I'll hit you again." He spoke as if talking to dogs.

"One. Two. Three..."

We rolled to our hands and feet, muscles quivering.

"Five. Six. Seven..."

We slowly stood, shaking.

He stared into our eyes with his dark gray eyes. "You're still defiant." Like lightning, he whipped the cattle prod between us, hitting us both.

We squatted, trying to keep control of our muscles.

"Stand up."

Again he stared into our eyes. "Less defiance. I want none. I can't take time to train you now. Go to the modeling room."

We went. I heard his steps behind us, and I asked, "What happened to Gronk?"

"No talking."

We modeled as usual. As we finished, I asked, Sally, "What happened to Gronk?"

"Oh, he's at the doctor. I'll be sure to tell him you missed him. How did you like Lurch? He's a new hire."

"Where'd you get him? A concentration camp guard?"

"Funny girl! He has a lot of experience as a prison guard. But he was fired for cruelty. Can you tell?" Sally smiled impishly, showing her perfect teeth between her perfect lips.

That night as we lay down in the dark, I said to Lulu, "Now what?"

"Sorry about that. I was sure we could overcome the guard. I never thought they had a cattle prod *and* a Taser."

"Yeah, I've never seen that before. When the Taser hit the pillow, I was sure we had him."

"I'm out of ideas." Lulu sounded defeated.

"I got one."

"What?"

"It may work no better than yours. How about we attack Sally and the guard during the modeling session?"

"One of us will get tased, and the other will get Sally. I like that!"

"Me too. Do you want to play rock paper scissors to decide who does what?"

"It should be me. You took point last time."

"You sure?"

"Yeah. Good night."

The next morning we both were completely humble and obedient to Lurch. Yet after staring into our eyes, he said, "You're still defiant. I promise I'll tase you for that. But not now."

Sally posed us in risqué swimming suits around deck chairs. I watched Lulu out of the corner of my eye. As Sally posed me and told me to look seductive, I heard the deck chair go flying. I watched Lulu as she landed on the Taser and take it in her belly.

Meanwhile, I grabbed Sally's hands and bent them both behind her. "Drop the Taser!"

Expressionless, Lurch held his Taser up for me to see the setting. "Let go of Ms. Bellows, or your friend will die. I've turned the power to zombie mode. That will kill her."

Lulu, jerking in pain on the floor yelled, "No!"

"Sally, get your goon to drop the Taser, or you lose two arms." I pulled her wrists up between her shoulder blades.

"Arghh! Drop it!"

"No." Drawing another Taser, Lurch shot me, and I fell to the floor. All I remembered was pain.

The door opened the next morning, awakening both of us. After hours of electrical torture, we'd fallen unconscious and were dragged and dumped in our rooms.

"Wakey, wakey!" squeaked a familiar high voice.

Every muscle in my body ached as I groaned, rolled over, and fell on the floor.

"Rough night? You've got ten seconds to stand. One. Two..."

I arose, shaking like a Parkinson's patient. Lulu quivered beside me.

"Gronk, you won't believe this," I said.

"Try me."

"I'm happy to see you."

"You're in bad odor now. You've got a day of torture ahead of you." He grinned.

We moaned.

"Here's your first surprise." Pointing the Taser at us, he reached to his eye and pulled off a brown contact. One red eye gleamed at us.

"What happened?" I asked, bewildered.

"Got zombified. It was the best way to treat my cancer. I have to hide it from Sally. You know she's got a phobia about zombies." He spoke conversationally, like he was a friend. He popped his contact back in.

"Get showered. You've got ten minutes for both of you."

Clean, awake, we felt better.

In the hall, Gronk said, "Turn to the right. We're going to the torture room."

We turned, then he said, "Stop. I think we should improve the odds a little."

"Ow!" I said as I felt a needle jab my buttock.

"Ay caramba!" Lulu said.

"Go to the end of the hall." As we slowly marched, Gronk said, "All the guards are in the torture room. There are nine, plus me. The guards will take turns until you're both groveling. The first one to get you to submit gets a bonus. I want that to be me, so when we get there, both fall to your knees and beg me to save you."

"You've got to be kidding!" I said.

"No way!" Lulu said.

"I just gave you injections of zombie blood. Guards are

watched as closely as you prisoners. If I'm going to bust out of here, I'll need your help. If we can stall until you're full zombies again, say twenty minutes, we should be able to defeat them all. Deal?"

"I don't know," I said.

"What have we got to lose, Sharon?"

"Uh, nothing. We've got no other plan. Okay, Gronk, we'll try it. By the way, what's your real name?"

"It's Elroy. I prefer Gronk."

"I understand."

"Sharon, I'm already feeling better."

"Yeah, me too." *Better* meant my whole body ached but I no longer felt shaky.

Gronk opened the door. Nine guards stood in a circle, each with a Taser and a cattle prod.

"Hi, fun lovers!" Gronk called. "Sorry to cut this play session short, but I persuaded these girls to submit to me. Right, girls?"

"Right." I fell to my knees and said, "I submit."

"I submit too," Lulu said next to me.

"Hey wait! That's not what the boss said," shouted a short black guard.

"We still want our fun," said another blond one who could be a model himself.

"I don't believe this," Lurch said. "Let me see their eyes."

"Look as long as you'd like, Lurch. I know how you love that," Gronk said. He folded his thick arms and smiled, looking like a furry frog.

Lurch peered into our eyes. They must not have turned red yet. I thought, *Submit, submit, surrender.* If we could just stall for ten more minutes.

"Something's weird about this. These are the two worst models." Lurch looked at Gronk. "You're the softest guard."

"Hey! I resent that," Gronk protested.

"Just facts. These Tasers record each use. You've used yours the least of all guards."

"If you think I'm so soft, Lurch, you just come here and say that to my face."

"I'll do that." He planted himself in front of Gronk and said, "You're soft." His nose almost touched Gronk's.

Thunk! Gronk's uppercut hit Lurch's chin, and he

collapsed in a heap. Gronk drew two Tasers and zapped the two closest guards. "It's time, girls!"

We went from kneeling to attacking with one snap of our legs and launched at the two closest guards. I head-butted mine and grabbed his Taser and cattle prod.

I heard the familiar CRACK of Lulu's flying kick and turned in time to see one guard slam into a wall, already unconscious. Lulu pivoted in air, twisted the nearest guard's cattle prod, and shocked him with it.

I jabbed the one next to me with a cattle prod and shot the one next to him with my Taser.

Gronk rammed into the last guard opposite him with two cattle prods, and the battle was over.

"Whew. I wasn't sure we could pull this off," Gronk said.

"It went really fast," Lulu said. "I feel like my old zombie self again."

"You are. Your eyes are glowing," I said.

"So are yours."

"Let's visit Ms. Sally and get out of here," Gronk said. "Go in front of me and keep your heads down. Don't let anyone see your eyes."

As we walked toward the modeling room, Gronk said, "Only Ms. Sally has the key out of here. The modeling room door goes to the guard's rooms, and only her key lets us out."

"Did you learn you'd be a prisoner after you agreed to the job?" I asked.

"You got it in one. Ms. Sally shows us how much money we have in the bank, but we never see any of it. She gives us anything we want, except freedom."

"I'm surprised no guard tried to escape," Lulu said.

"Some did, I think, but they just disappeared."

We entered the modeling room, heads bowed.

"Hsst! Why are you interrupting, Gronk? These two should be tortured," Sally said, looking furious.

Two models in eighteenth-century attire lounged on a divan.

"They've been tortured. Down, girls."

We knelt, heads still lowered.

"Well, well. You surprise me, Gronk. I thought you were the softest guard I had."

"I've toughened up. Look at this." Gronk reached up and

pulled his contacts off.

"Eeee! You're a zombie!"

"So are we." We jumped up and grabbed her arms.

"Eeee!"

Sally Bellows never stopped screaming until the police took her away to prison.

This is my darkest short story. I couldn't see any way to lighten it up. But I like to keep my readers on their toes with surprises, even dark ones.

Her Majesty's Corgis

by Andy Zach

Breeding zombie corgis wasn't all it was cracked up to be.

Heather Mallorn sighed as she reviewed accounts for Her Majesty's Corgis in Hanna City, Illinois. Certainly, she made plenty on each zombie corgi she sold. Normally, corgi puppies went for $1,200. She earned double that for zombies. The zombie corgies were invincible guard dogs, and cute too, with bright-red eyes. They were no harder to train than regular corgis, just slightly more aggressive. Well, a *lot* more aggressive.

She remembered when her corgis first turned zombie. One day there were fifty in her kennels, and the next they were all gone, with torn fencing in their wake.

Thanks to the undead mother-in-law, Diane Newby, Heather had gotten them back, and due to Diane's forceful methods, they were somewhat more obedient. That led to Heather's new career as a zombie dog trainer and breeder.

Zombies had moments of popularity, but they had the creepy factor that made people naturally averse to them, both people and animal zombies. It didn't matter the advantages of quick regeneration. This was part of her business problem.

For another downside, there were the expenses. Her zombie dog breeding insurance had risen again, the third time this year. That was because of recent claims: one pit bull eaten after it attacked a corgi and damage caused by corgis chewing through wooden fences. And after a car hit a corgi, the enraged animal attacked the tire, destroying a three-hundred-dollar radial.

Then there was the anti-zombie bias among dog breeders

and customers. Aside from supplying dozens of dogs to the Society Promoting Equality with Zombies, Heather's puppy sales were way down from when she just a normal corgi breeder.

This month she netted $15.73. Goody. She'd go out and buy herself a hamburger. Maybe she'd think of a way to make more money while at the local burger joint.

Munching on her hamburger, Heather watched a girl in a wheelchair, with a golden retriever service dog at her side. The kid dropped her napkin on the floor, and the dog immediately picked it up and handed it to her.

Huh. She wondered if she could make money by training service dogs. Having spent her monthly profits on a gourmet burger, she now studied service dogs on the internet.

Wow. She could make $15,000–$30,000 for each fully-trained service dog. That would take her from breaking even to successful, even comfortable. Plus, both the government and insurance companies would help pay for training. She was already training the corgis to not kill people. Picking up pencils and napkins would be easy. But she had to get a service dog–trainer certification first.

As Heather studied, she found it more complicated than she'd expected. The dogs' behavior had to be perfect in public and private under all distractions. She didn't know if she could get that from zombie corgis. But she had to try.

She started with her latest litter of Pembroke Welsh corgis. They quickly learned to pick up pencils, pens, and shoes. Training them to give them back took longer. Then teaching the zombie dogs to return items without chewing them to destruction took longer still. Zombie corgi puppies could take out a beef bone or a furniture leg in less than a minute.

After six months of training, Heather checked her dogs against the service dog requirements:

- No aggressive behavior—seven dogs passed.
- Cease sniffing behaviors unless released to do so—six dogs passed.
- No solicitations for food or affection—all passed.
- Overexcitement and hyperactivity in public—all passed.

She trained them to retrieve by pointing or by saying the name of the object. Three of her eight puppies could reliably do this. She called them Larry, Curly, and Moe.

Heather needed to place these dogs. Her business barely broke even. Her savings were gone, and she lived on her credit cards. She advertised her service dogs on the internet, the local newspaper, and through her own breeding and guard dog business.

No orders came in. She'd never considered zombie service dogs might not be desirable. Then her phone rang, playing, "Who Let the Dogs Out?"

"Her Majesty's Corgi's, Heather Mallorn speaking."

"Hello, do you have a service dog available?"

"Yes, I do. What are your specific needs?"

"I need the dog to get things for me and put them in my hand. I'm in a wheelchair."

"What kinds of things?"

"Everything. Stuff I drop, my clothing from out of my dresser, my slip-on shoes. My mouse."

"What specifically can you do, and what do you need the dog to do?"

"I'm a quadriplegic, wheelchair bound. I can grab things with my left hand, which I use to operate my computer mouse and my wheelchair joystick. My right hand and my legs are completely useless."

"Okay. What's your name?"

"Sandy Richards."

"And where do you live, Sandy?"

"901 Valley View Circle, apartment 1B, Bloomington, Illinois."

"Okay. It'll take a while for you to learn how to handle your service dog. I've got one ready to try out—Curly. When can I come over?"

"Wow! No one else said they'd come right away! C'mon over!"

"I don't live that far from you, and I've got the service dog ready."

"I'll be here all day. When will you get here?"

"Give me an hour."

Heather quickly put the service vest on Curly, which read, *WORKING SERVICE DOG—DO NOT PET.* Heather added a cummerbund she'd made for her dogs: *ZOMBIE DOG—DO NOT PET. NOT LIABLE FOR LOST BODY PARTS.* Her insurance company made her put these on all her dogs to prevent liability.

At the last minute, she remembered to take a pound of ground beef. Zombie corgis had an incredibly high metabolism. The only way to keep them under control was to feed them.

Heather and Curly arrived at Sandy's ground-level handicapped accessible apartment. Heather heard the door unlock after she rang the bell. The door opened, revealing a petite blonde in a pixie cut, smiling up from an electric wheelchair.

"Hi, you must be Heather," the blonde said.

"And you must be Sandy." Curly jumped up four feet to look through the window.

"And this is Curly. It seems he's eager to meet you."

"I'm eager to meet him!"

"Let me introduce you. Curly, this is Sandy."

Curly sniffed her outstretched hand.

"Sandy, this is Curly. He's trained to not lick or smell without permission."

"The vest says 'Do not touch.' Does that include me?"

"No. You're his assignment. Let me teach you his commands. As you work with him, he'll transfer his allegiance from me to you. Do you have a crate ready for him?"

"Yes. I bought one as soon as I started applying for service dogs. It's in the corner over there."

"Good. He's crate trained. That's his home base. Say, 'Crate.'"

"Crate."

Curly looked at Sandy and tilted his head.

"Use his name."

"Crate, Curly."

Curly trotted over to the crate, sat inside, and looked at Sandy, as if to say, *What next?*

"My, his eyes are certainly red. Why do zombies have red eyes?"

"They grow a layer of blood vessels in the eye that reflects light. This is why they can see in the dark."

"That would be handy early in the morning. Curly can get my slippers."

"Where are they?"

"In my closet."

"Curly, come." Curly trotted out, following Heather to the closet.

"Curly, slippers." Heather pointed at them, and Curly looked.

"Curly, take slippers."

Curly grabbed one.

"Give, Curly."

He placed it in Heather's hand. Then he did the same with the other one.

"Now you try it, Sandy."

"Okay. Curly, take slippers."

Curly looked at Sandy, then took the slipper from the floor where Heather had dropped it and trotted to Sandy. Sandy held out her one working hand, slowly opened it, and said, "Give, Curly."

Curly dropped the slipper into it.

While Sandy leaned over and put the slipper on her foot, Curly got the other slipper and waited for her to finish. When she opened her hand again, he placed the other slipper there.

"Good boy!" Sandy rubbed his head, and he wagged the bump that served for his tail.

"Here. Take this bag of ground beef. Give him a pinch."

Immediately Curly watched the bag of meat. Sandy pinched off a piece and tossed it. He jumped four feet in the air, snapped the morsel, somersaulted, and landed.

"This is wonderful! What else can he do?"

"Let me teach you all his commands. Be sure to keep him well fed. He gets a bit...aggressive if he's not fed."

"You know what would be really useful, would be if he could get stuff from the top of my fridge and from the high shelves in my closet. If I need something from there, I have to wait for my daily personal assistant."

"I think he can do that. What do you want from the fridge?"

"A bottle of water."

"Point to it and say, 'Take.'"

Curly's ears perked up at the word.

"Okay. Curly, take!" Sandy pointed with her skinny arm to the plastic water bottles on top of the fridge.

Curly zipped to the refrigerator and sprang up like a mole

in an arcade game. His momentum carried him upward, and he scrabbled onto the top. Grabbing a water bottle from the plastic wrap, he tugged it out and leapt off. He raced to Sandy and placed the bottle in her working hand.

"Fantastic!"

"Let's try all the other places you can't reach."

"Okay, the highest shelf is in the closet by the bathroom. There's not much room for a running start either."

"Try your command."

Sandy drove her wheelchair to the hall, pointed to the top shelf to a pile of clothing, and said, "Curly, take!"

Curly jumped to a shelf two-thirds of the way up, got his back paws on it, and jumped the rest of the way to the top shelf. He crawled onto the shelf, picked up the top piece of clothing from the pile, and jumped down. He gave Sandy the slightly soggy shirt.

"This is a dream come true," Sandy said.

"Great. Let's fill out your Medicare and insurance forms. I'll keep coming back here as long as you need help training Curly for any task."

After a couple hours of training, Heather returned to Hanna City, satisfied on multiple levels. Sandy had a useful service dog. They seemed to bond already. Medicare would pay Heather $9,000, and supplemental insurance would pay another $10,000.

* * *

Sandy went to bed tired but deeply satisfied. The dog almost seemed to read her mind. He was quick and eager to please. But he did eat more than she'd expected. He went through the pound of beef and ate five cups of dog food before he settled in his crate for the night.

The next morning a knock sounded on her door. She drove there and opened it.

"Hello," said a uniformed man. "I've got a parcel for you. Can you sign this?"

Curly growled.

"Curly, crate! Sorry. I just got him yesterday, and we're still getting used to each other."

"Uh, I'm afraid of dogs, especially zombie dogs. I can't

bring this in for you unless you lock him up."

"What could it be?"

"Um, the bill of lading says, 'Luxury dog home.'"

"Who would send me that?"

"There's no name, but the manufacturer is Lucky Dog Industries."

"Let me lock him up."

Sandy locked the crate while the delivery man brought in the large box.

"Let me unpack it for you," he offered.

"Thanks so much."

It was just a three-foot cube, like a fancy ice chest.

Reading the instructions, the man said, "I'll hook up the water, food, and air."

"Air?"

"Yes. This box is suitable for air shipping worldwide and keeping your pet in comfort."

"I don't have the money to travel worldwide."

"It's all paid for already. Maybe someone will give you a trip too."

"That'd be the day. I love to travel, but I don't know anyone rich."

"Okay, the food and water dispensers are working. Now let me try the air." He turned a valve, and Sandy heard a hiss. "Great. Let's test this out."

"Do you want me to let Curly out?"

"No. I'll test it with you." The man reached down, unlatched her seat belt, and picked her up in thick, strong arms.

"Wha-what are you doing?" Sandy could barely talk through her shock and fear.

"You're going to travel, just as you've always wanted." He placed her in the box. "Food, water, air. There's a litter pan too. Next stop, London!"

Sandy screamed.

"It's soundproof too." He put the lid back on.

"Curly, TAKE!" Sandy yelled with all her might.

Curly immediately launched himself at the cage bars. Bang! They bent but didn't break.

"Ha! Even zombies can't get out of steel cages, little dog," the delivery man said as he wheeled the box out the door.

* * *

Frantic, Curly bit at the bars. Snap. Snap. Snap. Again. Snap. Snap. Snap. He pushed and wriggled through the gap.

Curly looked at the closed door. Then he heard a truck start up outside. Without hesitation, he launched himself at the apartment window.

Blinds and glass broke as a thirty-five-pound superstrong corgi burst out the window like a dolphin leaping at a marine show. Curly saw the truck backing up.

Running as fast as he could, he leapt at the windshield. His hard head cracked it into a foot-wide star, but he bounced off. With a clash of gears, the driver squealed the tires and drove through the parking lot.

Gamely, Curly chased the truck and attacked the rear tire. His powerful jars clamped on the rubber, his needle-sharp teeth piercing it. Compressed air shot out his mouth. He rode the tire around and slammed into the ground. He didn't let go but worried the rubber and steel in his mouth.

Wham! Curly hit the pavement again. The air came out faster. Blam. He hit a third time, and with a whoosh, the remaining air rushed out. The tire was partly on and partly off the steel rim.

Turning onto the highway at high speed, the mangled tire came completely off. Sparks showered each time the rim hit the road.

Heedless of traffic, Curly chased the truck down the road. He knew he'd wounded it, but he had to get to the bad man in the cab. He jumped and landed on the side-view mirror. The driver quickly rolled up the window.

Curly scrambled onto the hood, scratching its surface to reach the broken-glass circle. The kidnapper's eyes went round and white as Curly dug through the broken glass to get inside. The man screamed as small paws burrowed through the glass, and he jammed his brake pedal hard. Three tires squealed, and one sprayed orange sparks.

Curly shot off the hood at thirty miles per hour and tumbled to the pavement. The driver gunned the engine and accelerated to crush the red-eyed corgi.

Seeing the truck bearing down on him, Curly ran *toward* it, jumped up, and crashed through the window. He bounced off the seat, then the dashboard, and then went straight for the driver's throat.

The bad man again slammed on the brakes, crushing the corgi against the wheel with his chest. Curly didn't let go of his throat.

Using his muscular arms, the kidnapper threw the corgi through the broken window.

Leaking blood like a freshly slaughtered pig, the driver wheezed, "No more of this crap. I don't get paid enough for this." He ran off.

Curly watched him, hesitating. He wanted to kill the bad man, but he knew his new master was inside this big box on wheels. He went around and around the truck, howling. He hopped into the cab. Then he heard some loud howling from outside.

He went out and saw a car with flashing lights and a loud howler stop behind the truck. He matched the siren's pitch and howled back. Maybe it was part of a pack? Then the sound stopped, but the flashing continued. A man in a uniform stepped out.

Curly ran to the man and wagged furiously. He led him to the truck and whined.

"You want to get in here, boy? You're all bloody! Let's see what this truck was carrying." The man opened the back of the truck.

Curly hopped up. There were several boxes inside like the one the man put his master into, but only one smelled of her. Curly went to it and began barking. He'd been trained not to bark, but this was too important.

"Something in this big box, eh?"

The man opened the box, and there she was! Curly jumped in and licked Sandy. Again, something he'd been trained not to do. But he couldn't help himself.

* * *

From the Bloomington Normal Sentinel

"Zombie Corgi Breaks Up Kidnapping Ring"

(Bloomington) A zombie corgi service dog in Bloomington, Illinois, broke up a kidnapping ring yesterday afternoon. After his master, Ms. Sandy Richards, was kidnapped by a man disguised as a delivery driver, the corgi broke out of his cage and jumped through the apartment window. Then he attacked the truck and disabled it. The corgi injured the driver and chased him away and then led the police to his master, who'd been stuffed into a sealed cargo box inside.

The police quickly captured the injured driver. He spilled the beans on the whole kidnapping gang. They kidnapped disabled people and sold them overseas for their organs.

The gang is in the Peoria county jail, awaiting trial.

We owned a corgi from 1996 to 2011. My daughter also owned one, so I know they're cute and assertive dogs. I enjoy writing about zombie corgis, so they got a short story in my anthology.

The next two short stories have mild spoilers for my middle-school science fiction book, Secret Supers.

The Secret Supers—Revealed

by Andy Zach

"Oh no! Did you hear what I just heard?" Aubrey said as soon as she and I rushed up to Jeremy and Dan coming off their bus in the morning at Maryville Middle School.

"No!" Jeremy said, rolling off the bus in his electric wheelchair. Jeremy Gentle was a spindly kid with cerebral palsy. I'd never looked twice at him when I was the most popular and smartest girl in the school. Then I lost my speech and balance to spinal meningitis last year, and I was put in the special-needs class. After we were together awhile, I learned he was as smart as me.

"Of course I *heard,*" said Dan, who walked behind Jeremy's wheelchair while holding the back of it and carrying his white cane. "Do you think I'm *deaf* as well as blind?"

Enough talking! I sent the thought to them all, using my telepathic power. *This is too slow! Our math teacher's car was stolen last night. Mr. Williamson went to play basketball downtown, and when he came out, his car was gone.*

I like my friends, but I wish they'd get to the point. We all attended a special disabled class at Maryville Middle School. Disabled kids used to creep me out. Now me, Kayla Verdera, was one of them.

Dan Elanga was the best-looking of the bunch. A dark West African immigrant from Cameroon, he was blind, but you couldn't see his eyes behind his dark glasses. I secretly hoped he'd notice me. That was silly, of course.

My best friend, Aubrey Wilcosky, looked at me like, "Why'd you interrupt?" Then she wiped my chin. I had trouble drooling since my illness. She'd stuck by me when I'd lost my speech and balance. I had been popular with "cool" kids in school—until I started using a walker.

We were opposites. On her artificial legs, Aubrey towered over me, big and burly, a kind of tomboy and athlete. I was small and thin. Aubrey could talk a knob off a door and was outgoing and friendly to a fault. I only talked when I had to—now I couldn't talk at all. I got all As, but Aubrey just muddled through school. She was a year older than us but in the same grade. She hung around with the sports crowd. I was in the honors classes. We became friends when I started helping her with her classes.

We stayed friends when Aubrey lost both legs in a car accident. She'd just been fitted for prosthetic legs when I got spinal meningitis. She didn't care I couldn't talk and drooled. She stayed in the special-needs class to get occupational therapy and partially to help me.

I still couldn't wrap my head around the fact I was one of them, probably for the rest of my life.

"Oh no!" Jeremy said, the last to learn about the theft. He was not telepathic like Dan and me but could move objects through his mind—telekinesis.

Jeremy had given us our superpowers. He loved playing with electronic gadgets, and his parents had supplied him a basement lab for experiments. When he discharged thousands of volts through super magnets, he'd knocked out the house's power and himself. Later, he discovered he had telekinesis.

Dan Elanga tried the same treatment but got partial telepathy. He could hear other people's thoughts and use their senses. After my treatment, I found I could project my thoughts and sensory impressions to others, but couldn't read their minds like Dan. Then Aubrey tried it and found her strength increased tenfold. She maxed out the weight machines at school.

"Mr. Williamson's wife had to come get him in her car," Dan said in answer to Jeremy's unspoken question.

"You read my mind!" Aubrey said.

Or mine!

"Or both of you. It's kind of funny. I follow a person's train of thought, and it's like a story unfolding. I pop back and forth so fast between your minds that I don't always know which thought I get from which mind."

"You should track that, Dan," Aubrey said. "It's good practice for you, and we may need to know who thought which thought when we're solving this case." Aubrey naturally led us. Or bossed us.

Are we going to be detectives, Aubrey?

"She certainly plans on it!" Dan said.

"Wait a second," Jeremy said. "We're just twelve- and thirteen-year-olds in seventh grade. How are we going to solve a criminal case? For all we know, the police will find the car before the school day ends."

"Don't be a doubter! Who has *special* abilities? Who can read minds? Dan. Who can make us disappear? Kayla. Who can make us fly? That's you, Jeremy."

"I can see where you're going, Aubrey. Is this like another practice to you?" Jeremy said.

Aubrey loved baseball. She had us practicing our powers daily on a baseball field in our neighborhood. That was where I discovered I could project the image of the ground in front of us to anyone looking at us and make us disappear.

"Nope, no practice. It's the opening game of the season!"

"We've got to go to our homerooms. Let's talk this over at lunch," Jeremy said.

* * *

Guys, I just checked the latest news on my tablet. The police haven't found the car yet, I thoughtcast to them as they headed to lunch.

My tablet hung on my walker and went everywhere with me. I used it to talk to people, picking out words on a keyboard and sending them to my voice app to speak them. I could pick any voice I wanted, and I used pop star Mackenzie Ziegler

Jeremy cautioned all of us not to reveal our powers to anyone, or we'd be in the center of a media circus. That was when Aubrey started calling our group the "Secret Supers."

I'm already here at lunch. I've got our usual table saved.

They walked to our table in the corner of the lunchroom and sat down. No one wanted to sit with us, so we had it to ourselves. My walker stood next to me. Jeremy could give me a support boost, so I didn't really need the walker if he was around, but I kept it to hide my secret identity.

I thought of something else too. We're going to need disguises.

"Can't you just turn us invisible, like when we disappeared from the boys at the ball field?" Aubrey asked.

We have to be visible to interview people. We can't just have Dan read minds. We're going to have to talk to people. And if we find the car, we'll have to talk to the police too.

"Also," Dan said, "it's easier to read a person's mind if they're thinking about your question. If it's something just in their memory, I can't read it, unless they call it to mind."

"Where do we start our investigation?" Jeremy asked.

"Right downtown, where the car was last seen," Dan said.

"That makes sense," Aubrey said.

"Haven't the police already searched there?" Jeremy looked at me.

Yes, but we can read the thoughts of all the neighbors.

"You mean, *I'll* do that. You know, that'll mean I'll have to read hundreds of peoples' minds," Dan said.

"It's good practice for you, Dan!" Aubrey said.

"Why is everything that's practice hard work?"

Our choir director used to say, "Practice makes perfect only if your practice is perfect." After losing my voice, I missed singing in the choir the most.

"How do you do that, Kayla? I can *see* the quotation marks!" Jeremy said. "I can practically hear his voice."

I don't know. I just think the quote, and out it comes. I have a good memory for voices and sounds.

"In any event," Aubrey said, "we need a plan to find the car. How do we get there? Jeremy, can you fly us downtown?"

"No problem. I can fly us all at about forty miles per hour. As the superheroes fly, that'll get us there faster than we can get in a car."

"Kayla, can you keep us invisible until we get there?"

Sure. Now about those disguises. How about we go as the Incredibles? We can buy the costumes at the costume store by my house. I thought they'd be good because they have masks and there're four of them, like us.

"Right, but what about copyright violation?" Jeremy asked.

"They're costumes, Jeremy! We're advertising for them," Aubrey said.

I thought about that too. They are no real Incredibles. Pixar

*owns the franchise. The costume maker paid a fee to make
them.*

"Uh, how much will this cost, Kayla? I don't have much
money," Aubrey said.

*Don't worry. My mom thinks it's a great idea, and she'll pay
for all of them.*

"I've got to watch that movie! I can see all of you loved it,"
Dan said. "Now that I can see through other peoples' eyes,
there's a lot to see!"

"Okay, back to our plan. We meet at my house as usual.
We go to the ball field as usual. We fly downtown invisibly, just
like we did yesterday. Then what? We talk to random people
around the gym?" Jeremy asked.

"Why not? Sometimes the direct approach is the best," Dan
said. "I'll be able to tell if they're lying or not and where the car
might be. That's a lot better than just picking the mind of every
person for blocks around the gym!"

"This might work," Jeremy said. "We can pose as
superheroes and say we're investigating the crime. People will
laugh at us, but they might help us too."

"I've been laughed at!" Aubrey said. "I've got that down pat.
Okay, let's do it! See you after school."

* * *

My mom had four packages ready in the car when she
picked us up after school.

"I think this is a great idea! This will make you incredible
children *really* the Incredibles!" Her dark eyes flashed as she
talked. I love my mom. She was dark haired and petite like me,
but her enthusiasm could overwhelm me.

"Mrs. Verdera, I hope my costume will fit me," Aubrey said.
"Dan is also extra large."

"That's what I got, two extra-large outfits and two smalls
for Kayla and Jeremy."

"I probably need an extra small," I said through my tablet.
"I'm smaller than Jeremy."

"Do you want me to custom fit the costume to each of
you?"

"Uh, I don't know. Let's try them on first," Aubrey said.

"If they don't fit, we can have you fix them," said my

computer voice. Sometimes it was handy, not having a voice that showed I was nervous about my mom finding out our secrets.

"Call me if you need me!" Mom said as we clambered out of the car at Jeremy's house. "Here's the bus now."

Jeremy rolled off the bus lift, and Dan followed him. "Hi, Kayla, Aubrey! Are those the costumes? I can hardly wait to try them!"

"I *see* they look great! Bright red. I can really get into this seeing thing," Dan said.

I'm so happy for you, Dan. Whose eyes are you using?

"Um, yours. And I'm happy for you, Kayla. And you, Jeremy. And Aubrey too!"

"I'm grateful too," Aubrey said. "And because of this great blessing, we *need* to use our powers for the good of other people, like Mr. Williamson. Let's try them on."

We descended to the basement. The boys changed in Jeremy's father's workshop, and Aubrey and I changed in Jeremy's lab. Then we met in the hall.

"I'm not sure about this fit," Aubrey said. The costume stretched tightly across her shoulders and chest as well as her hips and legs.

"Actually," Jeremy said, "it looks great. Skintight, just like the cartoon. I see Mrs. Verdera changed the Incredibles logo to *SS*. Now there's no trademark issue."

"Mine fits the same way, Aubrey. The fabric stretches. At first I was a little worried about it ripping," Dan said.

I have the opposite problem. Mine sags on me. Jeremy, you look like the only one with the perfect fit.

"I'll give it a try tonight. If it's too tight, I'll ask Mrs. Verdera to let it out," Aubrey said.

I'll definitely have my mom give mine a few tucks.

"Let's see what my mom says at supper," Jeremy said. "Dad's working late tonight."

As we ate lamb and rice, Mrs. Gentle said, "Yes, Aubrey's and Dan's suits are tight and Kayla's is loose. Too bad I don't have Mrs. Verdera's skill with sewing. The last time I tried to sew, I almost stitched my finger to a skirt."

"Ouch! When was that, Mom?"

"When I was about your age."

"We're going to go up to the ball field after supper."

"Will you play in your costumes?"

"Yes. We've got some team things to do there."

"Have fun!"

That was good dancing around the truth, Jeremy, I sent as our team arranged ourselves in Jeremy's flying car. After he discovered his telekinesis, he and Dan had built the car from wood and fiberglass. He told his parents it was an electric ground-effect vehicle, which was partially true. He had a car battery to power lights and instruments. With the car, he could use his powers publicly.

"Yeah, I don't want to lie to my mom. We'll go to the ball field, park the car, and then fly downtown. Invisibly, right, Kayla?"

Right.

Once at the field, we stood together with Dan and Aubrey in the back and me and Jeremy in front.

"Shields up!" Aubrey commanded.

"Um, no one's watching us," Dan said.

"I just like saying that."

It doesn't matter. I'm projecting an image of grass where we are on the field. I've got an image of cloudy sky ready.

"Take off!"

We soared into the sky.

We'll just look like a little cloud scudding across the sky.

'There are quite a few people below us, but I haven't found anyone looking up," Dan said.

I've learned to just blanket an area with a certain image in a certain spot, without really targeting any person.

"I've kind of learned to skim a lot of people's minds looking for one thing. Sort of like speed reading."

"That's great!" Aubrey shouted over the rushing wind. "You guys are getting more powerful. And, Jeremy, I think we're going faster than before! We're keeping up with the cars on the freeway."

"It doesn't feel any more difficult, but we're definitely going faster. The airspeed indicator on my augmented reality glasses shows sixty-five miles per hour!"

"Yeah, but we're going south, into the wind," Dan said. "Someone down there thought the wind speed was fifteen miles per hour."

Whee! I love this! I really feel like a superhero!

"You are, Kayla! We all are!" Aubrey said. "Now where's this gym, Jeremy? I know it's at Washington and Fourteenth Street, but everything looks different up here."

"That's okay. I memorized the route. We're following the freeway downtown, then we take the Washington Street exit. Fourteenth Street is by the baseball stadium."

"I'm glad you're driving!"

We saw the Maryville Stadium, where the city's minor league team, the Maryville Mayhem, played. We left the freeway and headed straight for the stadium. The gym sat next to it.

"Jeremy, don't land in the gym parking lot. Too many people are watching it."

"Where then, Dan?"

"There's a vacant lot around the block. Over there." Dan pointed with his hand. "Boy, that's weird. I was using everyone's eyes and I 'saw' it exactly, but when I pointed, I couldn't see it with my own eyes."

"There's a lot of weird things about our powers. I've broken lots of things since I got my superstrength. I tore a door handle from our car. Boy, was my dad mad! That's why I have us practicing our powers every day," Aubrey said.

We settled in the tall grass of an abandoned lot.

"Shields down!"

I cut our cloud cover when we got below the telephone wires.

"It's still good to say that! I feel like Captain Picard!"

We walked together to the gym. Aubrey took the lead, followed by Jeremy, then me, and Dan last. He touched my shoulder lightly, out of habit from following a sighted person. I didn't mind.

Jeremy used his power to support me and himself so we could walk without aid.

"Hi, kids," said the dark-haired, middle-aged lady at the gym desk. "Are you dressed up for some kind of play?"

"No, we're dressed for the real thing!" Aubrey said. "We're investigating the car theft a few nights ago, and we dressed up to hide our identities."

The truth is always the best! I had to strain to keep from laughing. My lips pressed together. I dabbed my lips with my handkerchief.

She laughed. "The police have already been here and

questioned everyone." Her name tag read *Miriam Busiri.*

"How about you?"

"Yeah, they talked to me. I was here yesterday evening, but we were busy with the basketball league and I didn't see the parking lot at all."

Dan reached over my shoulder and poked the tablet, punching out words, using my eyes.

She's telling the truth. I relayed Dan's typing on the tablet to them all.

"Okay, was anyone outside at that time?" Aubrey continued.

"Hmmm, only Khalid. Hey, Khalid!" she yelled into the gym.

A short, skinny, teenaged boy came running. "What's up, Mom?"

"These kids are asking about the stolen car. Tell them what you told the police."

"I came back from basketball practice at the middle school and got into the gym about 7:30 p.m. The car was still there."

"Did you see anyone in the parking lot?" Aubrey asked.

"Just some kids hanging around. They were on the other side of the lot."

Dan poked the tablet again, while Aubrey asked, "Did you recognize them?"

"Nope, never saw them before."

He's lying. He did recognize them, but he's afraid of them. He didn't tell the police either. I sent what Dan typed.

"Um, are there any gangs around here?" Aubrey continued the interrogation.

"Uh, yeah." Khalid looked down and shuffled his feet.

"Where are they?"

"I don't know. I try to stay out of their way."

He's telling the truth there. Oh, Dan's got a picture of the teens from Khalid's mind. He thinks he can recognize them, using our eyes.

"Okay, thanks for your help, Khalid. Ms. Busiri, do you know about any gangs around here?"

"Yeah, but you shouldn't mess with them. They've got guns, and they're not afraid to use them."

"Where are they?"

"I don't know what you're playing at, but I'm not going to

get you in trouble. They'll come out at night and sell drugs. Get off the streets before then. Where do you guys live? I've never seen you here before."

"Oh, up north. Thanks for your help. We'd better be going then."

"Be safe, kids! Don't mess with any gangs!" she hollered after them.

As soon as we were outside, Dan said, "She thought of the gang the 'Washington Wizards.' They harass shop owners and shakedown pedestrians for money when they're not fighting other gangs for turf or dealing drugs."

"I guess that means we'll walk down Washington looking for them," Aubrey said.

"She also thought of their headquarters a couple blocks to the west. There's a bar and a martial arts studio."

"Sorry to be a party pooper, guys, but do we really want to risk our lives? Shouldn't we call the police?" Jeremy asked.

"The police probably already know about them and probably already talked with them," Aubrey said.

"But what about us getting shot? Isn't this kind of stupid? We aren't invulnerable!" Jeremy said.

"No, but we can defend ourselves and disarm them. If they pulled a gun on us, can you get it out of their hands before they shoot it?" Aubrey asked.

"Uh, I guess so. I could flick the safety on, and they couldn't shoot it."

I can make us look like the ground beneath us. That'll make us hard to hit!

"And I can tell you if the person really will shoot or if they're bluffing. And if there's anyone hidden with a weapon," Dan said.

"So there, Jeremy. We've got our plan."

"I've got a bad feeling about this!"

"You just want to quote Han Solo."

"Well, yeah."

"So you can be Han Solo and I'll be Picard!"

That's so messed up!

"Hey, that guy over there is a member of the Washington Wizards gang!" Dan pointed across the street.

"Let's question him!" Aubrey looked both ways and ran across the street.

"We might as well run across now too," Jeremy said.

We jogged after her. Jeremy half lifted me, so I bounced like I was on the moon.

"Hey, you!" Aubrey strode up to a teen in a black hoodie emblazoned with *Wizards* in red. He wore dark glasses and scowled at Aubrey.

"What kind of getup is that, girl? Are you some kind of gang on our turf? Get the hell out of here!"

"I guess we're a kind of gang," Aubrey admitted. "We're just investigating the car theft from the gym yesterday."

"Are you deaf? I'll beat your ass if you don't get off our turf!"

He's nervous. He knows about the theft and where the car is! I relayed Dan's typing.

"Oh, c'mon." Aubrey looked him squarely in the eye. "We know the Wizards stole the car. Do you want to hand it over, or do you want us to call the police?"

"That's it!" He whipped out a switchblade and held it to her throat.

Aubrey grabbed his wrist. SNAP! His wrist broke. Simultaneously, the blade flew from her throat into Jeremy's hand.

Then the gang member ripped his glasses off and yelled, covering his eyes with both his hands. "Yow! My wrist! My eyes!"

I projected an image of the sun into his eyes.

"Sorry about that. I didn't mean to break your wrist. Here. Let me put it in a splint." Aubrey pulled his wrist straight and bound it to two branches she'd torn from a tree.

"Who the hell *are* you guys?" the kid groaned.

"We're the Secret Supers. We're superheroes."

"Kid superheroes?"

"Why not? Now, are you going to tell us where the car is?"

"Okay. I'll take you there. It's in a garage a couple of blocks away."

It's a trap! Kayla sent to them after Dan whispered in her ear.

"Is the car really there, or are you trying to trick us? Maybe we should just call the police."

"No! Don't call the police. The car's really there. I drove it there last night."

He's telling the truth. But it's still a trap. There are other gang members there. I sent them what Dan whispered in my ear.

"Okay, lead the way. I'm Aubrey. What's your name?"

"Jimmy."

"It's simple, Jimmy. We get the car, we call the police, they get the car, and we disappear. If you give us trouble, we give you trouble."

"Let's get this over with."

That's a double meaning! He means to get rid of us! I liked teaming with Dan. Together we made a complete telepath. And it gave me a reason to hang with him.

We marched our captive a couple of blocks off Washington into a run-down neighborhood. He led us down an alley, where we saw an old-fashioned garage with big swinging doors. A padlock secured the doors.

"I think that used to be a carriage house," Jeremy said.

"You got the key, Jimmy?" Aubrey said.

"I hafta go get it."

He's going to get the gang!

"You do that. We'll wait right here."

He left.

"The gang's house is across that street!" Dan said.

"Then let's get the car out." Aubrey grabbed the lock and ripped it and the hasp off the wooden door. "That felt good." She flung open the doors, revealing Mr. Williamson's car.

"I've practiced driving in my parents' drive. I can back it out of here," Aubrey said. She sat in the driver's seat, and we piled in. The ignition had been popped out and hotwired.

"Just push these wires together," Jeremy said. He did, and the car started. "I'll call the police."

We drove into the alley.

"Here they are!" Jimmy called. "Now you're in for it!"

Four young men in Wizard hoodies surrounded the car, each pointing a gun at us.

"Get out," the leader said. "I don't want your blood all over the car."

"And what'll you do when the police get here?" Jeremy asked.

"They'll be busy looking at your bodies. We'll be long gone."

"Guys," Dan said. "There are two more gang members in

the house with rifles on us."

"Idiots! They're supposed to stay hidden," growled the leader.

"Drastic times call for drastic measures," Aubrey said, slowly getting out of the car and holding up her hands. The others all opened their doors and slid out.

"Watch out for her!" Jimmy said. "She knows some kind of karate."

"Execute escape plan!" Aubrey shouted. She disappeared, followed by Jeremy, Dan, and me.

They can't see us now! I'm projecting the image of the street where we are.

"He's going to shoot!" Dan shouted, crouching near the car door and pointing at the leader.

My mental images affected just those on the street and in the house. We could see each other.

All four guns flew into the air and into the tree above the street.

"What's going on? Where'd they go? What happened with our guns?" The leader looked around wildly.

"This!" Aubrey shouted as she felled him with a mighty punch. She bounced to the next startled gang member and knocked him out too. The others started running. She easily caught up to them and took them down.

"Oh, good idea, Kayla!" Dan shouted.

"What's going on?" Jeremy asked as a police siren sounded in the distance.

"She's blinded the guys in the house! She's just projecting what *I* see. They're blind as bats, and they're panicking and stumbling all over the house!"

Does that mean I can cut our invisibility shields now?

"Yeah. No one is looking on the street. The neighbors are hiding."

Whew! That was hard! Six different images to six different people.

"But you did it!" Aubrey shouted. "Here are the police."

"What's going on here?" asked the first officer as he got out of the car. "Did you have some sort of gang fight?" The second followed, two hands on his unholstered pistol, pointing down.

"Well, yes, sort of—" Jeremy said.

"No!" Aubrey said. "We found this stolen car, and this gang

tried to take it from us. They pulled guns on us."

"Wait. Start from the beginning. How did you find this car, and why do you think it's stolen?"

"It's our teacher's car, and he said it'd been stolen," Aubrey informed him. "We asked the people at the gym, and someone saw kids hanging around the gym yesterday. We heard about the Wizards gang and saw one on the street. We said we'd call the police if he didn't show us the car."

"The license plate matches the stolen vehicle from yesterday," said the second officer.

"Okay, I'm glad you found the car, kids, but what about these gang members on the ground? How'd you knock them out without getting shot?"

"I punched them!"

"I distracted them!" I said through my tablet.

"Me too!" Dan added.

"I took the guns," Jeremy said.

All true! Nice job!

"Your story is unbelievable."

"Even incredible!" Aubrey said.

"You'll have to come into the station for complete questioning," said the first officer.

"Execute escape plan!" Aubrey said.

We vanished. A puff of wind blew dust into the street. No one looked up and saw a small cloud speeding across the sky.

* * *

The next morning, Aubrey and I greeted Dan and Jeremy as they got off their bus.

Did you hear the news last night? They said four vigilante kids playing superheroes caught the Wizards gang with a stolen car.

"Uh, sorry, Kayla. What's a vigilante?"

Sorry, Aubrey. A vigilante is unofficial, unauthorized law enforcement.

"It was used in the Old West for posses that went after criminals," Jeremy said. "Really, any superhero is a vigilante."

"Spiderman? Batman? Superman?" Aubrey said.

"Yup," Jeremy said.

"I've got to catch up on my comic reading," Dan said. "I see the pictures in your heads, but I sense a lot of background that I don't know."

"Hey, today let's just read comics after school!" Aubrey said. "We need a day off after yesterday. Everyone bring your comics collection. Dan, you can read our minds."

"I like your plan! We can all discuss the comics around the dinner table! Your mom's making grilled salmon tonight, with teriyaki sauce!"

"I swear, Dan, you know more about our meals than I do," Jeremy said.

"You read comics; I read minds for meals!"

This is an excerpt from my middle school novel Secret Supers. It's the first time the four seventh graders use their superpowers.

A Hamster's Tale

by Andy Zach

How fascinating! Dancer thought. *This book says there are libraries where hundreds of books live. It also says the fiction books are in order by author name.*

Dancer scurried off *Your Sixth Year Reader* to look at Jeremy Gentle's bookshelf again. Jeremy was Dancer's owner and unknowing educator. Ever since he'd taught himself to read by studying the newspapers lining the bottom of his cage, Dancer had craved reading.

He hadn't figured out why he'd started reading. One day he'd noticed patterns in the markings. He saw they repeated themselves in clumps. He saw the clumps formed more patterns. He also listened to his owners differently. They also spoke in patterns. "Jeremy" was always called "Jeremy" or "Jeremy Gentle" by his mother, and sometimes by his father.

Dancer had learned to understand Jeremy and his parents, and then he'd put the terms they said with the clumps on the paper. Each letter had a sound, and together they formed clumps his master called "words." The idea was brilliant. No wonder they were his owners and he was only a hamster.

Dancer read each paper eagerly to the point of memorizing it, but reading started to bore him. Jeremy only changed the lining about once a week. So he'd watched Jeremy open and close his cage door. Then he copied the motion, using his paws and nose. He left to search for more words to read.

He found a treasure trove. This bookshelf was one of six in this lower level of the master's big cage. He'd explore upstairs when he finished the books down here. He wasn't even done with this shelf yet.

The books he read so far were Jeremy's old school books, all marked up by Jeremy. Dancer could smell Jeremy's scent on them. He'd learned about books called "fiction," which were stories humans invented. Humans organized fiction by author, not topic, like nonfiction. Now, he'd look for these fiction books.

He scanned the shelf above the school books. Some of the hardbacks had names on the binding. Those were the authors. Wells, Yellen, Zach. That was alpha—maybe these were fiction. He climbed to the second shelf and pulled the Zach one— *Zombie Turkeys*—out of its place.

Soon he was engrossed, and he hardly heard the front door open. Jeremy was home! He had to get back in his cage. Using his paws and mouth, he jammed the *Your Sixth Year Reader* and *Zombie Turkeys* back onto the shelf and scampered across Jeremy's lab. He shinnied up the table leg to his cage, flipped the sliding door up with his nose, and squeezed in.

Jeremy rolled into the room in his electric wheelchair, with his friend Dan Elanga.

"Hi, Dancer! You're up to greet me! Look, Dan. He's standing up against his door."

"He does look like he's greeting you."

Jeremy picked up Dancer and petted him. Dancer smelled Jeremy's familiar scent. Someday he'd have to tell Jeremy that he'd learned to read. But how?

This Andy Zach seemed to know a lot about animals, at least zombie turkeys. Maybe he'd give Dancer some ideas.

After Jeremy and his parents left the next day, Dancer finished *Zombie Turkeys* and learned about zombie squirrels, rabbits, cows, and people. They were weird, but not any weirder than what he read about people in the newspaper. Humans did all kinds of crazy things. He didn't even know if *Zombie Turkeys* was fiction or not. Or was the newspaper fiction? Nothing was marked. There was so much he didn't know.

Dancer noticed a contact email for Andy Zach in his book. He climbed Jeremy's computer desk. He'd played with the computer once before and found it confusing. Now he had a purpose. Send an email to Andy Zach.

The hamster pushed the mouse with his front paws until

the arrow on the screen was over the circle with the three colors, then he clicked it with his nose. A window opened. He had seen Jeremy do this to send an email many times. *Now, what did he have to click next?*

He read everything on that window. Bookmarks, 120 unread, News, My Drive, Blog. *Hmmm…120 unread what?* He clicked on it.

Mail. He'd found it! Now, how to write one? Again he read everything. A rectangle with one word, "Compose." *That meant to write music. Could it mean write an email? Words often had more than one meaning.* He clicked it.

The window changed. It now showed:

From: Jeremy Gentle

To: (blank rectangle)

Subject: (blank rectangle)

Then there was a big blank space. Another rectangle with the word "Send" appeared at the bottom.

Dancer breathed faster, like he was racing on the wheel in his cage. *This is it!* Carefully, he placed his paw on each letter on the keyboard: andyzach@andyzach.net. That was Andy Zach's email address.

He had to push the mouse and click to go to the next rectangle. Subject: "how do i tell my owner i can read?"

That didn't seem quite right, but he couldn't think of any other way to put his question. Andy was an author. He should be good with words.

What should Dancer say to Andy? Just tell him the truth.

andy,

i'm a hamster. i learned to read. how do i tell my owner, jeremy gentle? i can't talk. please help.

dancer

That seemed to cover everything. The letters weren't quite right since he couldn't figure out how to capitalize, but it probably didn't matter. He pressed Send and went to read the rest of Jeremy's bookshelf.

As he spun his wheel that evening, Dancer thought, *How will I know if Andy responds? I suppose the unread emails will go to 121. I'll just have to check in the morning.*

Jeremy and his parents closed the front door the next morning, and Dancer raced out of his cage to the computer desk. Opening the window, Dancer saw 123 unread emails. He scanned them. One subject read, "To Dancer, care of Jeremy Gentle." From Andy Zach. That was for him! He opened the email, twitching his whiskers with eagerness.

Hi Jeremy and Dancer,

If this is Jeremy reading this email, read the attached email and you'll understand. It's from your hamster, Dancer.

If this is Dancer, pay close attention.

Your email fascinated me. Proceeding on the assumption this is not a hoax, here's what I recommend.

First, keep reading and learning about the world of humans. No matter how much you know, it isn't enough. We're weird and dangerous.

Second, you'll have to wait until I finish my *Secret Supers* book tour. Then I'll come to Maryville and personally introduce you to Jeremy and his friends. I'm sure they'll be happy to meet you and be friends.

Third, if you want to keep this secret, delete this email after you read it. Don't send me any more. Jeremy can read them.

I look forward to meeting you, Dancer!

Your friendly paranormal animal author,

Andy Zach

Where was the Delete button? The hamster moused around the screen, hoping for a pop-up instruction. He went over a rounded rectangle with lines. "Trash" appeared. He clicked it, and the email deleted.

Whew! Computers puzzled him. But Dancer hoped Andy would know what to do with Jeremy and his parents. He had plenty to learn while he waited. He'd caught up to Jeremy in English. What subjects should he try next?

There was this group of books called "Encyclopedia" on the bottom shelf of one of the bookcases. He'd avoided them because they were so big and heavy. But he'd just learned the meaning of "encyclopedia" in Jeremy's seventh-grade English book. It meant a collection of books that contained all knowledge. That was what he needed.

Too bad he couldn't read an encyclopedia on the computer. He didn't think he could put the big book away. He scanned the screen again for "encyclopedia." Nothing. But what was this blank area with a round symbol? He put the mouse arrow over it, and the word "Search" appeared.

Carefully he typed "encyclopedia" in the blank, then clicked the symbol. A new window popped up. "Free encyclopedia online" it read.

"How long do book tours last?" he typed.

He read several articles, with no clear answer. *It seems some questions don't have clear answers.* Some authors never stop touring. Some do it for weeks or months. Too bad he didn't ask Andy how long he'd be on tour.

Under "Popular Topics," he saw "Abraham Lincoln," a name Dancer recognized from Jeremy's school books. He began reading. He had a lot of learning to do.

* * *

Lincoln was interesting, and his history showed how dangerous humans could be. As a break from the violence, Dancer read about hamsters. There were seventeen types, or species. They lived in Europe, Asia, and the Middle East.

The world was enormous. What he could see out the windows was the least of it. Dancer felt an urge to explore his neighborhood. How long did he have before Jeremy returned? He glanced at the clock. Twelve thirty. He had four hours.

He'd learned to tell time from Jeremy's first-grade math book. Once he'd gotten past addition and subtraction, he'd been confused, but clocks were a great invention of humans.

Dancer went out the doggy door, followed by Jeremy's black lab, Diesel. He sniffed Dancer curiously and then went about his business.

Dancer explored the backyard and then slipped easily under the gate in the fence. He loved the fresh air and exploring—What was that?

A small striped animal ran up to him. Dancer concentrated and remembered the word for it...chipmunk. It looked like the picture in Jeremy's book. Except this chipmunk had a metal cap on its head. Odd.

After staring at him, the chipmunk ran off as fast as it'd arrived. He'd have to ask Andy Zach about this when he saw him.

Dancer completed his circumnavigation of Jeremy's property and returned through the doggy door. Diesel raised a sleepy head as Dancer entered, and then the dog lay back down. Dancer felt proud, a little like that human Magellan he'd read about. Maybe later he'd have a chance to go around the world with Jeremy.

But now he was tired. He reached for Andy Zach's next book, *My Undead Mother-In-Law*, and snuggled up for a good read. The story talked about human zombies and their problems and adventures. Then rats and snakes, monkeys and chipmunks appeared with "metal yarmulkes." What were those?

Back to the computer Dancer jogged. He learned a yarmulke was a small cap worn by observant Jews. Judaism was one of the many religions humans followed. Was Andy writing about Jewish animals?

He'd never thought about religion himself. It was just one of the many things people did that he didn't understand. He trotted back to the book. What did Andy say about these animals with yarmulkes? Was the chipmunk he saw one of them?

Frantically he read more of Andy's book. There it was. The metal yarmulkes indicated cyborg-controlled animals. Another online dictionary check taught him a cyborg was a part-human—or animal—part-machine combination. In Andy's book, a criminal controlled the cyborg animals.

Does that mean some criminal is was using the chipmunk to spy on Jeremy? That'd be terrible! Now he knew real fear. Humans had always seemed so powerful, but when they turned to evil, they were dreadful. There was only one thing he could do. Back at the computer, he typed:

dear andy,

i found a cyborg chipmunk outside jeremy's house. i'm afraid it's controlled by a criminal. what should i do? please answer quickly.

dancer

He sent it and returned to finish Andy's book before Jeremy returned.

* * *

"Hi, Dancer," Jeremy said as he rolled into his downstairs science lab, where Dancer lived.

Dancer stood up against the cage and waved his paws.

Jeremy seemed to like that.

"You've really got waving down. I've never seen a hamster do that before." Jeremy reached into the cage and picked him up.

Dancer wriggled his whiskers as he looked at Jeremy. Jeremy liked that too. If only Dancer could talk.

"Sometimes I think you almost *can* talk," Jeremy said. Then he sighed and put him back in the cage.

Jeremy wheeled over to his computer. Dancer watched him carefully. He opened a window and clicked on his emails.

"So many emails. I think I'll just delete them all," Jeremy murmured to himself. "What's this? Andy Zach wrote to me!" Jeremy read the email aloud.

"Dear Jeremy,

I'll stop by Maryville tomorrow on my book tour. I'll appear in your local bookstore and then at the high school in the evening. Could we get together for supper, with your family?

Call or text me.

Your friendly paranormal animal author,

Andy Zach"

"Hey, Mom! Guess what?" Jeremy shouted into the intercom on his desk. He drove to the elevator in their house.

Dancer heard it go upstairs. He wished he could hear what was going on upstairs. Maybe he could. It was risky, but Dancer felt reckless. He shinnied down from his cage and climbed up to Jeremy's desk. Jeremy had installed an intercom between his lab and the kitchen. Dancer turned it on.

"...and so Andy Zach will be here tomorrow and wants to eat with us." Jeremy's voice came out of the speaker.

"To treat him, we should take him to some fancy place to eat," Mrs. Gentle said. "He wrote his book *Secret Supers* about you and your friends."

"Don't you remember when Andy was here in Maryville, writing *Secret Supers*, Denise? He loved your cooking better than any restaurant in town," Jeremy's dad said.

"But what could I make?"

"Just your popovers with roast beef, carrots, and mushrooms. He liked that the best."

"How do you remember what he liked? I mostly remember him asking all these questions about Jeremy and his friends when he was writing about them."

"*I* remember what *I* like, and he liked the same things I do."

"That makes it easy then. I'll thaw the roast and get it ready for tomorrow evening."

"I'll call him right now!"

Jeremy seems excited, Dancer thought.

Dancer returned to his cage and hopped onto his wheel. He needed to think about how to communicate with Andy Zach tomorrow. Dancer thought so hard, he forgot to eat. But he couldn't solve his communication problem. Maybe Andy would have some idea.

* * *

Dancer awoke when he heard Jeremy and his family scurrying around the house upstairs. This wasn't a school day, yet they were up early.

He returned to the intercom and turned it on. He heard rustling and clattering, then—

"I've got breakfast ready. When did Andy say he'd be here?" That was Jeremy's mother's voice.

"Any minute now. It's five to eight," Jeremy said.

"His bookstore appearance is at ten," Jeremy's dad said. "Ah, that might be him."

"Hi, everyone! Jeremy, Bradon, Denise."

So that's what Andy sounds like. His voice was a little deeper than Jeremy's dad.

"Thanks so much for having me over, not just for breakfast, but supper tonight."

"It's the least we could do after you wrote your book about Jeremy," Mrs. Gentle said.

"Whatever made you turn their story into a science fiction one, with superpowers and everything?" Jeremy's dad said.

"I thought the story of plucky disabled seventh graders would reach even more kids if they were superheroes. It seems to be working. Sales have been good on the tour."

They settled into breakfast and boring conversation. Then Dancer heard Andy say, "I have an unusual request for you, Jeremy."

"What's that?"

"Could I take your hamster, Dancer, as a good luck charm

with me to the bookstore?"

"Uh, of course. Whatever you want, Mr. Zach. I'll make sure the cage has food and water and a fresh newspaper."

"I'll have to leave soon. I want to get to the bookstore by nine to set up."

"Okay, I'll go down now."

"Mind if I go with you? You can introduce us."

"Sure. C'mon."

Dancer turned off the intercom and returned to his cage. He stood against the door and waved as they entered the lab.

"There he is, Mr. Zach. See, he's waving at you!"

"My! How friendly. Mind if I pick him up?"

"No. That'll help me as I get the cage ready."

"He certainly looks like an intelligent hamster."

"Yes, he's been standing and waving at his door to greet me the last week or so."

"Can you think of any reason why?"

"Um, not really. We got him for me. Our dog, Diesel, is really Mom's dog, who trained him. I said I wanted a pet of my own, and Mom and Dad got me this hamster. He's been good and friendly since I got him. He didn't even mind when I experimented on him."

"That was when you tested your superpowerful magnets on him?"

"Right. I knocked him out twice."

"Those same magnets that gave you and your friends their superpowers, right?"

"Yes. That was really clever of you to tell our story, including our superpowers, yet make everyone think it's fiction. You both told the truth and hid our superpowers."

"Thanks. Did it ever occur to you that your hamster might have gotten a superpower?"

"Uh, no. He's just a hamster. His brain is less sophisticated than a human brain. I wouldn't expect it to react at all the same."

"You're right. I would expect something completely different."

"Like what?"

"Let me show you something." Andy turned on Jeremy's computer. Then he opened a window.

"Dancer, what would you like to say to me and Jeremy?"

Andy asked. He placed Dancer next to the keyboard.

Slowly, carefully, Dancer typed:

hi jeremy. hi andy. i learned to read and write. i'm so glad you know now.

Then Dancer turned, wriggled his whiskers, stood up, and waved his paw at them.

Jeremy's mouth hung open like a zombie's. Andy said, "Jeremy, Dancer had previously written two emails to me telling me this. He also told me he saw a cyborg chipmunk around your house, like the kind the arch-criminal Sid Boffin used to spy with, as I told in my book *My Undead Mother-In-Law*. I think this room is secure, with all the electromagnetic shielding you've put in it, but I dare not talk about this more in public. The NSA is looking for cyborg animals in Maryville even as we speak. I'll take Dancer with me and let him type on my laptop to tell his story. How's that sound to you, Dancer? Wave if you agree."

Dancer stood and waved as hard as he could. He was finally getting a chance to talk to Jeremy. He'd have to thank Andy too.

"I don't know what to say," Jeremy said. He turned to his hamster. "I'm happy for you, Dancer. I guess you're a member of the Secret Supers now too. We certainly can't let people know you're a genius hamster. But would you like to be our Secret Supers mascot?"

Dancer stood and waved.

* * *

Andy set up his book display at the bookstore Secret Garden of Good Reading. He carefully placed Dancer's cage under the display table out of sight. He slid the laptop into it, turned it on, and opened the word processor.

"Here you go, Dancer. Tell us everything you can of what you remember and how you learned to read and write. Click on this square to save your work. You could lose all your typing if you don't," Andy said.

Dancer began typing. His heart raced. This was more exciting than the hamster wheel or even Andy Zach's books. He was writing his story.

He wrote everything he remembered. How he began to

understand human speech and writing. He realized for the first time that he had no memories before a certain point. The first thing he remembered was listening to the patterns of human speech and how he heard the same sound from Jeremy each morning. The words fell into place after that. "Dancer," his name, then "Jeremy," and "wheel," and "cage," and all the others.

A little time passed, and then Andy said, "How are you doing, Dancer? Would you like some fresh air?" Andy carefully removed his laptop and put Dancer's cage on the table.

"Oh, he's so cute!" said a middle-aged lady next to the table.

"I brought him from Jeremy Gentle's house for good luck today, Mrs. Duckworth," Andy said.

"Oh, call me Gladys, Andy. He's certainly been lucky! This has been one of our best author appearances."

"I'm glad, Gladys. I'm always happy to meet fans and to sell books."

"I've brought some sandwiches for us for lunch," Gladys said. She handed him a wrapped bundle.

"Thanks. Mind if I share the lettuce with Dancer?"

"Of course not. We've got to keep our lucky charm happy."

Andy gave him a piece of lettuce. It was a nice break from Dancer's usual fare. After lunch, Andy returned the laptop to the cage and Dancer got back to work. He told about meeting the cyborg chipmunk, writing emails, meeting Andy, and going to the bookstore.

He stopped. There were *so many* books to read. He could spend the rest of his life in the bookstore.

That brought him up to now. What should he write next? *That's it. I'll ask all questions.* There were quite a few.

Andy lifted up the table skirt. "Time to go, Dancer. We're done here."

Wait. He thought of one more thing to ask. Quickly he typed, "what's the nsa?" Then he clicked Save.

Taking the laptop, Andy glanced at the last question. "That's a good one. I'll tell you in the car."

Andy put Dancer's cage on the passenger seat. "Okay, Dancer. 'NSA' stands for National Security Agency. They're the nation's agency that investigates international communications from terrorists and criminals worldwide.

According to the texts I've gotten from them, they've located the cyborg animals' control center. I've got to make a call on my NSA secure phone to talk to them."

Andy took out a red phone and dialed it. "Hi, General Figeroa, what do you have for me?... You've found the control center in West Hampton? Great... Ah, you're sending in Diane and the Paranormal Privateers? They should be able to take care of it... Oh, there's a house here in Maryville you want *me* to check with the Secret Supers? I'll talk to them... Will do. Bye."

Dancer was a little concerned. The Secret Supers included his owner, Jeremy. He didn't want him tangling with any criminals.

"Hmmm, Dancer. I'd better call Jeremy's friend Kayla Verdera. She can communicate to them all using telepathy. We need the Secret Supers help right away." Glancing at him, Andy frowned. "I'd swear you look worried. Here, type out your concerns while I call." Andy put his laptop into Dancer's cage.

Dancer was glad to tell someone about his concerns. While he typed, he listened to Andy's call.

"Hi, Kayla, this is Andy Zach. You can broadcast to me... This is an emergency. Can the Secret Supers meet me at Redwing street here in Maryville?... That's great. See you in five minutes. Wear your uniforms. This is an undercover operation. Thanks. Bye."

"Okay, Dancer, let's see what you think of all this." Andy took the laptop back.

"why does jeremy have to be involved in catching criminals?" Andy read.

"Jeremy and his friends are actually very good at catching criminals using their powers. Haven't you read *Secret Supers* yet?"

Dancer shook his head no.

"Jeremy has telekinesis, Dan can read minds, Kayla can broadcast thoughts and sensory sensations, and Aubrey has superstrength. They have more trouble with school than criminals."

Andy continued reading. "will jeremy and his friends be in danger?"

"No, I don't think so. They aren't expecting us, and we can use Dan to scout them out. The NSA thinks it's only one or two people here running the cyborg animals in town out of this house on Redbird street. And here we are. And here come the Secret Supers."

Andy picked up Dancer and put him on his shoulder. Down the street flew a bright-red flying car with a bubble top. Jeremy drove, and he had a small girl with dark hair next to him. Dancer recognized her: Kayla Verdera. In the back were two big kids. One was Jeremy's best friend, Dan Elanga. He had a round, dark face and black hair, and dark glasses because he was blind. The other Dancer knew as Aubrey Wilcosky. He couldn't forget the six-foot-tall girl with two prosthetic legs.

Aubrey jumped out of the car first, bouncing on the strong springs of her artificial legs. "Hi, Mr. Zach. It's been a long time since we've been on a mission. Where's the gang you want us to get?"

"Aubrey, they're down the street a ways. Mr. Zach wants me to listen in on them and scout them out," Dan said as he got out.

Jeremy and Kayla floated out of the front seat and then walked to them. Jeremy used telekinesis to help him and Kayla walk when fighting crime. Kayla usually used a walker. She had bad balance and couldn't talk.

Dancer had seen Jeremy float around the lab using his telekinesis, but not in public before. Then the hamster noticed the four seventh graders had red uniforms with "SS" on them and black masks. He supposed this would fool most humans, but he could tell who they were by smell.

"Okay, Dan, the address is 323 Redwing, four houses down on this side of the street. What can you tell us about the people inside?" Andy asked.

"Hmmm. There only seems to be one, and he is...watching us! He's got a TV monitor, and the camera is in the grass, not too far away!"

"I wonder if that's the chipmunk Dancer saw, spying on us now?" Andy said.

Hearing the word "chipmunk," Dancer stood on Andy's shoulder and waved.

Jeremy laughed. "Dancer thinks so."

"Can Dancer tackle the chipmunk, and then we can attack the house?" Aubrey asked.

"Dan, what defenses does the house have? Can you tell?" Andy asked.

"The owner's pretty confident. He's waiting for us to attack. Oh no! He's got cyborg black mambas over the doors! And rats. And a monkey. And a gorilla!"

"Rats," Andy said. "That's pretty much how Sid Boffin fought the Paranormal Privateers. We may have to wait for them to come here."

"I think we can take them," Aubrey said. "Kayla can blind the guy, and then he can't direct his cyborgs."

Right. I just project darkness, like Dan sees, into his brain, Kayla thoughtcast.

"Only I can now see, using other people's eyes when I read their minds," Dan said.

"What if we don't go in the doors, where they expect? What if we go through an open window?" Jeremy said.

"I suppose you can fly through it," Andy said. "And surprise is your best tactic. Okay, let's give it a try. Aubrey and Jeremy can lead the assault through the window. Dan will read your minds, and Kayla will give everyone an update on what's happening. But first, Dancer, can you go and grab the chipmunk? That'll surprise the controller. Then Kayla can blind him. He won't know you're going through the window." Andy put Dancer on the grass. "Can you do your part, Dancer?"

Excited to be part of the team, Dancer stood, nodded, and waved his paw.

"Let's do it!" Aubrey said.

"Everyone huddle up around Dancer," Andy said. "Dancer, you slip off through the grass and find the chipmunk."

Dancer scurried off.

"I'm watching him," Aubrey said. "He's making a beeline for the yard next door. Or is that a hamster line? Ooo! He's tussling with the chipmunk! He's got him pinned. Strike the controller blind, Kayla!"

Done!

"Oh, he's panicking now," Dan said. "He's punching controls and trying to do things blindly. He's dropped the mambas by the doors, front and back. The rats are also prowling there."

"Let's go, Jeremy," Aubrey said.

Like a middle school Superman and Superwoman, Jeremy and Aubrey flew to an open side window. The screen popped off, thanks to Jeremy's telekinesis, and he flew in, then Aubrey.

"They went into the bathroom," Dan said. "Tell them to go to the basement, Kayla. But that's where the gorilla is! Jeremy is putting the rats and the mambas into the freezer upstairs."

"Will they be able to handle the gorilla?" Andy asked.

"Jeremy thinks so. His telekinesis can lift over a thousand pounds. And so can Aubrey," Dan said.

"Tell them the gorilla probably is confused without directions from the controller," Andy said.

I'm relaying all of this to them, thoughtcast Kayla.

"The blind controller is just pushing one button over and over. It's the gorilla's attack signal!" Dan said.

"Hey, where's Dancer?" Andy asked.

I saw him slip into the house through the cat door, thought Kayla.

"They're downstairs," Dan said. "The door to the control room is locked. Aubrey kicked it open. And the gorilla attacked! Aubrey slugged it, but it didn't slow him down. Jeremy has it pinned on the floor, but he can't hold it. It's slowly moving toward them, like a zombie. They're dodging, but the gorilla's not stopping, and they're not giving up. It's an impasse. They can't get past the gorilla."

"Oh no! Jeremy's getting tired. The gorilla's moving faster. Wait. What's that? Dancer is there! The gorilla doesn't notice him. Jeremy just yelled to Dancer to chew through the power cord to the computer. Dancer stood and waved and went inside."

"Kayla, can't you blind the gorilla?" Dan asked.

No. My telepathy doesn't work on animals.

"Nor does mine," Dan said. "I can't read Dancer's mind. Oh, now the gorilla has slumped down. Jeremy and Aubrey have gotten in. Aubrey's tying up the controller. Poor Dancer. He chewed through the computer's power cord, and he's lying on the carpet. Jeremy's doing CPR with his telekinesis. He's really frightened. He wants us in there. I'm going in!"

Dan, Andy, and Kayla rushed into the house, raced down the steps, and found Jeremy and Aubrey huddled over Dancer. Jeremy was crying.

"Is he all right?" Andy asked.

"I-I-I-don't know," Jeremy said.

Lying on his back, Dancer opened his eyes, waved his paw, and closed them again.

This is the second tale from Secret Supers. Think of it as an extended epilogue.

Caribbean Cruise

by Andy Zach

"Arrrgh! Me hearties, eat hearty!" said a short, stocky pirate with an eye patch and a captain's hat seemingly copied from Cap'n Crunch. The pirate gestured, with a hook instead of a right hand, toward an enormous banquet table laden with food. The one visible eye gleamed red.

"Arrrgh! Where's the skilly and duff?" said a refrigerator-sized bald pirate with an enormous mustache. His eyes also shone crimson.

"Arrrgh! That be the tacos and enchiladas," said a small, beautiful pirate with dark hair bound by a red bandanna and smiling blood-red eyes. She pointed with her cutlass toward the Mexican section of the smorgasbord.

"Arrrgh! You be a Mexican pirate?" said a blond pirate with broad shoulders and a Cockney accent. She wore her hair in a long queue emerging from a bloody headband around her forehead. She also had glowing ruby eyes.

"Aye, you be right, matey. You be a limey?"

"Aye, right off Blackbeard's ship. You?"

"Lately from the Spanish Main."

"We be goin' thur agin'," growled the behemoth.

"That be so, Cap'n?" queried the beautiful dark brigand.

"Aye, Lulu—oh no! I slipped."

"You're the first one to break character, Diane. You're out," said the huge man in a now American midwestern accent.

"What's a suitable punishment for our captain?" asked the blonde, using an easy Oxford accent.

"I'm not really the captain. That's Captain Koumondoros. But I'll wash the dishes," said the pirate captain, sounding like a middle-aged woman.

"Mrs. Newby, the crew'll take care of that," said a serious-looking man in a real captain's hat. His eyes were a normal brown. "You enjoy your zombie launch party."

"I think the cap'n should walk the plank—over the swimming pool," said the small pirate, her eyes twinkling.

"I second that, and I'm her husband. I know she has her swimsuit on under her costume," said the mustachioed pirate.

"All right, George, but you have to take off that horrible mustache. And that skin cap."

George tore off his fake mustache but hesitated with the skin cap. "Diane, it hides my gray hair."

"Oh, you're not that gray. It just makes you look distinguished."

"Since we're decostuming, let me take this off." The blonde removed her bloody bandage. "That was hot."

"That's right, Sharon. You Brits can't take the heat," jibed the small brunette.

"Yes, over twenty-five Celsius is too hot for us, or me at least. But you Mexicans don't like the cold, Lulu."

"Sí. I get cold below seventy. It feels good to be out of the pirate talk," Lulu said in her lilting Mexican accent as she walked toward the pool, behind George and Diane Newby.

"It's all the same to me. Just one more accent or language," Sharon said in Spanish.

"That's what I like about you. You speak Spanish like a Mexican."

"Or a Castillian," Sharon said, switching to that Spanish accent.

"Or any of your other twelve languages," Lulu said.

"We each have our strengths. I learned a lot about martial arts from you."

"I was an MMA fighter for a couple of years."

"And a cliff diver in Acapulco."

"We're he-re!" Diane yodeled as she entered the pool deck. "The ship cleaned up nicely, Captain Koumondoros. It was a wreck the last time I saw it, when we defeated Sid Boffin's crime empire."

"Thank you, Mrs. Newby. But the military did most of the repairs. The crew just added some polish."

"The pool looks beautiful, and the ship feels so still. If it weren't for the breeze, I wouldn't know it was moving," Diane said as she shed her pirate costume and climbed the diving board. She filled her swimsuit like the middle-aged woman she was.

"We're making a steady twenty-two knots," the captain said.

"That's twenty-five miles per hour, Diane," George put in.

"Thanks, dear. Here goes!" Diane bounced high off the board and did a credible swan dive into the pool.

"Well done!" Sharon said.

"Mrs. Newby, do you want to try Acapulco next?" Lulu asked with a smile.

"Why not?" she said from the pool. "New experiences, like this shakedown cruise, are what I live for. Let's try this." She dove to the bottom of the pool.

"What do you think she'll do?" Lulu asked George.

"With Diane, you never—"

WHOOSH! Diane shot out of the water like a missile and landed on the pool deck dripping wet. Her feet slipped, and she smashed into the deck butt first.

"Diane! Are you okay?" George asked.

"The only thing injured is my dignity. Let's go to the bow, George. I want to reenact the Titanic scene."

"Now I've seen your zombie superstrength, I'm impressed," Koumondoros said.

"Hah! That's nothing. Wait until you see us regenerate," Lulu said.

George had to trot to keep up with his wife. "Diane, you're running like a schoolgirl."

"George, I'm so happy. We defeated the supercriminal Sid Boffin, and then the president gave us a letter of marque and Boffin's superyacht. We get to sail around the world fighting criminals!"

"True, but there'll be danger and discomfort, I'm sure."

"As zombies, we've already had our danger and discomfort. How many limbs have we lost and grown back?"

"I've lost track."

"That's what I like about being a zombie. You get knocked down, but you always get back up."

Diane climbed the railing on the bow. George held her ample waist in his enormous hands. Diane spread her arms wide.

"I'm flying!"

"You look just like the ship's figurehead."

"George, that was so sweet of you to get a figurehead made of me. It even has red eyes behind the cat's-eye glasses. But it makes me look too good."

"In my eyes, you look even better."

Diane leaned backward, and they kissed.

* * *

"Let's go, George! We've got a shakedown cruise to shake down." Diane stood up from the breakfast buffet in the dining salon on the fourth deck of the ship *Resolute Too.*

"What do you plan on doing?"

"This checklist the captain gave me has him testing various speeds up to the top speed of twenty-eight knots. That's at ten this morning. I want to be there."

"Let me finish my pancakes and we'll go."

George gobbled down his stack of wheat cakes smothered in maple syrup and butter. Then they climbed the wide marble stairway to the salon deck.

"Look how beautifully the stairs cleaned up," Diane said as the ascended to the salon deck.

"Last time I saw them, they were covered with blood and bull dung."

"I'm glad our zombie bulls survived the fight. I'm fond of my bull, Whip."

"And I like my bull, Durham, too."

The couple walked through the formal Italian salon and forward toward the bridge. They could see the helipad decks looming up behind them.

Captain Koumondoros stood behind the pilot as they entered. He turned his square, brown, weather-beaten face and said, "Welcome, Diane and George. I thought you might come here for the speed trials."

"I'm eager to see what this baby can do!" Diane said.

"I am too. We haven't gone over our cruising speed since we left New Orleans."

"Aren't the engines over twenty thousand horsepower?" George asked.

"Yes, almost twenty-two thousand, before the military modifications."

"I didn't know about that," George said.

"I was briefed about them. They put superchargers on all four diesel engines. The theoretical maximum is now twenty-five thousand horsepower."

"Theoretical? Don't you know?" Diane asked.

"No. Not until they're at sea and we test the superchargers under real conditions. From the maximum speed, we can compute the horsepower delivered."

"Let's test them then."

"Pilot Stavrinides, you may go to full power."

"Aye-aye, sir." The pilot eased the throttle from cruise to full power.

They felt a steady vibration through their feet, like driving over rumble strips.

"Is that vibration the engines?" Diane asked.

"No, the engines are in the outer hulls of the trimaran. We can't feel them here," the captain said. "We're feeling the gulf chop. Look. We're now up to twenty-seven knots. That's the fastest I've ever sailed before."

"I know you were the captain of a container ship. What else have you sailed?" George asked.

"A variety of cargo ships and a fishing sloop in my youth in Greece."

"I'm a little disappointed," Diane said. "I thought those superchargers would do more."

"Oh, we haven't used them yet. They're a new addition, so there's a special switch for them. Kostos, switch on all four of the superchargers."

"Aye-aye, sir." He flipped four new switches next to the throttle.

The pitch of the thrum increased and then faded slightly.

"Why did the vibration decrease?" Diane asked.

"We're hydroplaning, riding the surface of the water. I never dreamed a fourteen-thousand-ton vessel could plane. Look." He gestured toward the speedometer. "Our speed is up to twenty-nine and a half knots."

"That's impressive," George said.

"What's that? Thirty-four miles per hour? We do that in my old Taurus all the time," Diane said.

"But your Taurus doesn't weigh fourteen thousand tons, Diane," George said.

"Nor is it going through water," the captain said.

"Plus, the energy required to power increases with the square of the speed. From twenty-seven to twenty-nine and a half. That's..." George punched rapidly on his calculator. "About twenty percent more energy."

"So in horsepower, we're delivering..." The captain punched his own calculator. "Twenty-six thousand three hundred and seven horsepower."

"Captain! The surface radar detects something off our bow," the radar operator said.

"What is it?"

"It's too small of a reflection for a boat but too large for a fish. Maybe a whale."

"Oh, don't hurt it!" Diane said.

Captain Koumondoros picked up a pair of binoculars and looked at the horizon.

"There it is! It's trying to get out of our way. Cut the superchargers and reduce speed to cruising," he ordered.

Looking again, he said, "It looks like a very small submarine cruising on the surface. Hmmm. Call the nearest Coast Guard vessel," he directed the communications officer.

"Why the Coast Guard?" George asked.

"I think it's a drug runner. It's a semi-submersible boat that's mostly underwater. The Coast Guard needs to know."

"Can't we take it down? Arrest them?" Diane asked.

"That's not really our mission on our shakedown cruise, Diane. Remember what General Figeroa of the NSA told us before we left: 'Follow the plan. Keep a low profile.'"

"Of course keep a low profile—with a five-hundred-foot luxury yacht! I like our NSA liaison General Figeroa, but I didn't really take that seriously. And anyway, orders have to go by the board when there's an emergency like a criminal drug runner."

"Captain, we'll pass the sub on our starboard bow," Pilot Stavrinides said.

"Captain, the nearest Coast Guard vessel is two hundred miles away. They'll be here in ten hours," said the comm officer.

"We can't let them get away!" Diane said.

"We can't ram it. And I'm not going to turn the ship around," Koumondoros said.

"They're breaking the law. Thousands of people will be hurt by those drugs. We can't do nothing. Our letter of marque says we can take action." Diane pulled a piece of paper from her purse and read: "The President of the United States authorizes and commissions, under this letter of marque and reprisal, the privately armed and equipped persons and entities as, in his judgment, the service may require, with suitable instructions to the leaders thereof, to employ all means reasonably necessary to seize outside the geographic boundaries of the United States and its territories the person and property of the enemies of the United States."

"Realistically, Diane, what can you do? I'm responsible for the ship and its boats, and I'm not chasing the sub. You can't get on board the sub without them."

"Oh yeah? Watch me!" She turned and ran out of the bridge, ripping her clothing off, revealing her bathing suit underneath.

"Diane!" George chased her to the starboard railing.

"George, I dove off this ship with a hole in my chest and survived. This'll be a cinch!" Diane jumped to the top of the railing and dove off into the ocean eighty feet below, in between the ship and the passing sub.

"No!" George jumped after her into the gulf.

Diane transferred her vertical speed into horizontal speed and closed quickly on the sub. She added zombie strength to her dolphin kick and popped out of the water like a seal, onto the deck of the sub, just a foot and a half above the sea.

George shot out of the water after her, looking more like a walrus, landing on his stomach.

"Diane! What are you doing?" George yelled over the sound of the water rushing by them.

Diane ran to the small conning tower and tried to pry open the hatch. It didn't budge.

"Open up, you! In the name of the law, in the name of the United States!" Diane pounded vigorously on the hatch.

"What will you do if they open up and they have a shotgun?"

"Take it from them."

"And if you get shot?"

"Meh. I've been shot before. I can regenerate."

"Surrounded by salt water spray? You know that kills the zombie bacteria."

"Hmmm. That may be a problem. Oh look! The ship is turning around."

They could see the ship's profile as it turned to the starboard to give chase.

"Look. There's the ship's launch," George said. The ship's forty-six-foot boat emerged from the stern transom dock and sped toward them.

"We'll get you!" Diane yelled at the hatch, still beating it. "We've got help coming!"

In response, the semi-sub increased its speed.

"I don't think they can outrun our boat and our ship," George said.

"Look ahead!" Diane said.

A small green-covered island lay ahead of them.

"I don't recall any island in the gulf here," George said.

"Maps don't have everything."

"Here comes the ship's boat," George said.

The white bow wave made a V in front of the deep-hulled craft. It slowed and matched the sub's speed as it came alongside them. Lulu and Sharon leapt onto the deck of the boat. Each held a yard-long crowbar.

"Oho! I see you have an entry key," Diane chortled.

"You forgot one when you left so quickly," Lulu said.

"Let's see if they open now," Sharon said. She walked to the hatch and banged on it. Lulu joined her.

"Open up! Abra la puerta! Ahora!" Sharon yelled.

"I forgot they're probably Spanish speaking," Diane said.

"Here, George. You're bigger than me. Put those football muscles to good use." Lulu gave him the crowbar.

George wedged his bar into the hatch. Sharon put hers in next to his. She was the next biggest zombie after George, slightly taller but nearly a hundred pounds lighter.

"One, two, three!" they said together, and they threw their weight into the bars.

The hatch bent, and both bars slipped out.

"Okay, let's repeat that," George said. They put their bars at either end of the bent hatch.

"Hey, look how close the island is," Diane said.

"Are we going—" began Lulu, then all four zombies flew into the water as the sub grounded to a halt on a sandbar.

Lulu came up spitting water. "Ay caramba!"

George and Diane kicked up together.

"Well, they're not going anywhere," Diane said.

"I hope our boat and ship avoid that sandbar," George said.

"Look. The boat is swerving, and the ship is slowing, slowing, stopped," Diane said.

Sharon popped up. "I took a look around the sub to see if they were scuttling it or dumping their cargo. Nothing. We've got them trapped."

The hatch burst open, and a bedraggled, bearded man chattered in Spanish while waving a shotgun at them.

"He says, 'Don't move. I've got you covered,'" Lulu said with amusement.

"Let's see if he does," Sharon said as she slid beneath the water.

"George, let's pretend we cowed, while Sharon gets behind him," Diane said.

"Okay, but let's edge toward the beach."

George, Diane, and Lulu, hands aloft, slowly waded ashore. A second man climbed out, carrying a submachine gun and yelling in Spanish.

Lulu translated, "He said, 'Don't follow us, or you'll be shot on sight.'" The men ran into the heavy jungle past the beach. The zombies saw Sharon trot after them and gesture *follow me*.

"Race you to the jungle, Diane," George said.

"A jungle adventure! Chasing drug runners. It's like a second honeymoon."

"With me as a chaperon," Lulu laughed.

Their headlong dash immediately slowed. Vines and thick undergrowth impeded them. The sound of the surf faded. They could hear faint sounds ahead but could see nothing.

"This may be harder than we think," George said. "Diane, Lulu, if we get separated, head to the beach and circle back to the sub."

"Let me scout ahead. I'm smaller, and I can slip through more easily." Lulu quickly moved in front of George. "I can see their tracks—Oh!" There came a heavy thump. Got you!"

"Got what, Lulu?" George asked as he caught up to her,

Diane close behind. Looking down he saw a snake with its head crushed by Lulu's crowbar.

"This'll be harder indeed," he said.

"Charge on! We weren't stopped by sandbars. We won't be stopped by snakes," Diane said.

The three pursued the drug runners.

"Whew! This is hot work," Diane said. "I'm getting cut by thorns, but my skin regenerates in a minute. How are you two doing?"

"I can still see a faint trail. If they don't leave a trail, I'm sure Sharon is leaving broken branches for us to follow. We've come about a mile. And it is hot, even for a girl from Acapulco."

"Only a mile? It seems a lot farther to me," Diane said.

"It's slowgoing, especially if you're widening the trail," George said. "The island can't be more than a mile across. We must be circumnavigating it."

"Sì. I've heard and smelled the sea a couple of times to my right. We're going counterclockwise around the island."

A couple of gunshots rang out in the jungle.

"That's a shotgun," George said.

"I hope Sharon's all right," Diane said.

They rushed through the jungle. Then Lulu, still a dozen feet ahead of them, called back, "And there's Sharon, safe and sound."

They saw Sharon sitting at the base of a tree, looking at her arm.

"Safe and sound? I suppose so," Sharon said. "I caught the fringe of a shotgun blast and I'm still healing. See?" She pointed to a raspberry spot on her arm. A shotgun pellet erupted from her skin, like a blackhead, and fell to the ground. The red area decreased in size as they watched.

"Where are the drug runners?" Diane asked.

"One is up this tree. They separated, and I followed this one. He took two shots at me from the tree."

"Let's go up and get him," Diane said.

"I've got an idea," George said.

"What?"

"Let's go back to the ship and get the zombie corgies. They can track the last guy."

"I'll keep watch here," Sharon said. "I think he's out of ammo. There are no trees nearby. I'll be the coon dog and he's the coon."

"It'll be faster if we make for the beach and run back to the ship," said George. "This clearing seems to lead there."

"Race you!" Lulu yelled.

The three zombies took off at nearly thirty miles per hour. They saw the boat and the ship just two minutes later.

"Yoo-hoo!" Diane yelled to the boat. "Take me over to the *Resolute Too*. We need the zombie corgies." Still in her bathing suit, she immediately swam to the boat offshore and climbed the ladder in the stern.

George and Lulu waited onshore until Diane returned in an inflatable zodiac raft, accompanied by ten zombie corgies and the pilot.

"Okay. Back we go to Sharon!" Diane said as she took off at a run.

The three friends met Sharon a few minutes later, trailing a pack of yipping corgies.

"Ah, reinforcements," Sharon said. "No word from our treed prisoner."

"The corgis should be able to track down the missing miscreant," George said.

"But first we've got to get this guy down the tree, to give the corgis the scent. Poor dogs, having to smell him. He's no bed of roses," Diane said. "I picked up a pair of handcuffs from the MPs on board." She brandished them.

"I've always liked climbing," said Lulu. "Up, up, and away!" She jumped four feet up and then shinnied up the tree.

"Look at her go," George said.

"She really climbed the cliffs at Acapulco when she was a teen," Sharon said.

They heard yelling at the top of the tree, a struggle, and then Lulu cried, "Look out below! Man down!"

"Let's see if I can catch him," George said. "I can hear him bouncing from limb to limb as he falls."

"I'll help. We can make a basket," Sharon said.

They linked arms, grabbing each other's wrists. Then they maneuvered to where the falling sound was above them. First, the empty shotgun landed. Next, they saw the man hit a limb about thirty feet above them, grunt "Oof!" and then flop off.

"Gotcha!" George said as the arboreal drug runner landed in their linked arms.

The man was unconscious and looked like he'd been in a vicious street fight. He was filthy, his clothes were torn and dirty, and scratches covered him from his head to his bare feet. The corgis gathered around, sniffing and licking him.

"I don't think he's up to walking to the boat," George said.

"We can carry him just as we caught him," Sharon said.

"Good idea," Diane said. "Lulu and I can chase down the other guy with our corgis. They've got the scent now. Heck, even *I* could smell him."

"See you back at the ship, Diane," George said.

"Bye! Okay, pups, go get your druggie."

"Let's backtrack our trail and find where the other guy split off," Lulu said.

"Ugh. I didn't like that the first time. George warned me serving our country might be uncomfortable. Maybe it'll go faster this time."

The corgis kept their noses down along the trail and widened it. One corgi yipped as a snake struck it. Immediately, the other nine attacked the snake and devoured it in seconds.

"Weren't they fed today?" Lulu asked.

"Yes, but they're always hungry. And they take attacks very personally."

"Look. They're splitting off the trail."

A marshy spot turned out to be a tiny stream, which the corgis followed. Their speed increased, and they yipped, like hounds on a fox's tail.

The stream ended in a spring-fed pool that nourished a small tree. In the tree was the other drug runner.

"Cuidado! Vete, dispararé!" he said as he brandished a submachine gun.

"He's going to shoot!" Lulu yelled.

"He's in for it now!" Diane ran to the tree and jumped halfway up to the first branch.

Lulu climbed on the other side. The corgis jumped four, six, eight feet high, scrabbling up the tree.

The submariner began spraying them wildly with bullets. A corgi dropped to the ground. Lulu took shots in her shoulder and hip. A lucky shot hit Diane in the head.

"Oooh..." She sighed softly as she fell to the ground twelve feet below.

"You're in trouble now!" Lulu yelled in Spanish.

"I've got some for you too," the man growled, swinging the gun to cover her.

Too late. A corgi reached him and ripped out his hamstring. He sat heavily on the branch. Lulu jumped on him and tore away the gun. Another corgi tore the man's Achilles tendon.

"Yow! I surrender...I surrender. Just save me from these dogs!"

"I should let them have you." Lulu twisted his arm behind him. "Dogs! Sit!"

Ten dogs sat, arrayed on various branches, like strange red-eyed birds. They quivered with eagerness. Their mouths drooled with desire for fresh meat. Two dogs had bloody muzzles.

Lulu saw Diane sprawled on the ground near the pool. She could see the bullet wound right in the middle of her forehead. It had already clotted shut.

Looks like I'll have to get this creep down myself. Lulu tied his hands together in front of him using the climbing rope she carried on her belt. *It's amazing how often this has come in handy.*

"Off you go." She pushed him off one side of the branch and jumped off the other side. He outweighed her, so he slowly descended while she went up. Lulu played out the line and hit the ground when he did. He screamed as his legs collapsed.

"You stay there," Lulu said with grim humor as she checked on Diane's head. No exit wound. The entrance wound was nearly healed. She wondered how the zombie bacteria would handle a closed-head injury.

George and Sharon came crashing down the trail.

"We heard the shots," George said. "Wha—Diane!" He cradled her head in his lap.

"She caught one in the head. The bullet's still in there. What will happen?"

"We've recovered from worse before. Usually the bullet— what's this? There's a bump on the back of her head. Ah." His hands worked in her brown hair, streaked with blond highlights. He peeled something off the back of her head, covered in blood and hair. He held it up.

"As I was about to say, bullets usually work themselves out as the zombie bacteria heal and replace our tissues. This one had to work its way through her skull."

"She's tough. When will she wake up?"

"The bacteria double in quantity every twenty minutes, replacing whatever tissue is necessary. It's been twenty minutes already. Anytime now." Continuing, George said, "That's our bad guy? What happened to his legs?"

"The corgis got him before he surrendered."

"Couldn't have happened to a nicer guy."

"George?" Diane moaned.

"Yes. I'm here, Diane."

"What happened? I remember climbing the tree, then nothing."

"You caught a bullet. In the head."

"Again? I hate that."

"It's all right now. I'll carry you back to the ship."

"I'm okay now." She sat up. "Do ya got something to eat?"

"I've got an MRE," Sharon said.

"Anything'll do. I'll clean up at the smorgasbord back at the ship. I've got the healing hunger."

Diane ate the MRE, and they all returned to the boat. George carried the captured drug runner.

They returned to the *Resolute Too* and washed and treated the drug runners. The Coast Guard cutter showed up to take the prisoners.

As soon as they saw the guardsmen who came aboard, the criminals knelt and pleaded in Spanish. The officers and Lulu and Sharon laughed.

"What'd they say?" Diane asked.

Still laughing, Lulu translated, "Please arrest us! Put us in prison! Get us away from these zombies!"

Now this short story is a prequel to Paranormal Privateers. It is a story I cut from the draft of that book.

The last short story takes place after *Paranormal Privateers.* It
doesn't contain too many spoilers.

We've Got It!

by Andy Zach

    "Okay, that's it, Tom," my dad said.

    "What's it?" I asked.

    "You've got until next week to move out."

    "Um, where will I live?"

    "That's your problem, isn't it? Try the local apartments. Look for rooms to rent on the internet. It's not that hard to find a place in Ohio."

    I could tell by his grim expression he was serious this time. He'd been nagging me for nearly a year to move out and "set up housekeeping" ever since I'd graduated from the state university with my BA in video game art and my minor in computer science. I'd managed to wheedle him out of it and delay the date. Until now.

    I'd been saving money from my Game Stop job to move out, but I kept dipping into it to add to my video game equipment. I had a sweet system, the fastest I could afford using the latest alien technology. Oh. I needed to find someplace to keep all my equipment too. And I needed internet access—high speed. I had to have at least a gigabit-per-second speed, or I couldn't keep competing.

    This might affect my standing in the Fortnite league. My stomach clenched in worry. I texted my best friend, Nick.

    Gotta talk now. R U free? - T

    Gimme 5 minutes - N

    I spent five minutes inventorying all my computer equipment: hyper-reality goggles, high-speed desktop/flat-screen combo, quadraphonic earbuds, five gps Wi-Fi modem, and my motion sensor. I grimaced. I wanted a whole-body VR suit that gave touch, heat, and motion sensations, as well as read them, but I couldn't afford it.

While the aliens still controlled the earth, their VR headsets broadcast all sensory input into our brains. Boy, those were sweet units! They gave an unparalleled game experience. However, since the aliens also used them for mind control, the government banned them as soon as the Paranormal Privateers took over their mothership. Ever since, the gaming companies have been trying to replicate the experience. The VR bodysuit came the closest.

Still, what I had was superfast. The Lorain city Wi-Fi was only a couple hundred gigabits, but my parents had upgraded to ten gigabits per second. My dad had a programming job with one of the flying hoverboard manufacturers in town. He wanted me to get a programming job there, but I still had hope of becoming a professional gamer.

My phone rang. "Dude," I answered

"What gives?" Nick said.

"I gotta move out this week."

"Whoa. Where you going?"

"I don't know. Do you know any places?"

"Let's see what's online."

"Doh. Of course. I'll look too."

"First one to find a place wins."

"Wins what?"

"Free pizza."

"I can taste it now," I said.

"Lame. I've got a place for eight hundred a month here in town."

"What's the Wi-Fi situation?"

"No mention. Probably city."

"That's a no-go. I need at least a one-gigabit connection."

"What's that cost? Fifty bucks a month?"

"Yeah, but I can barely afford eight hundred."

"How about if I move in with you?"

"I didn't know you were moving out."

"My mom's always complaining about how much I cost her. It'd be nice to be on my own."

"Ooo! I found a place for only four hundred a month."

"What kind of dump is it? Mine's a two-bedroom

apartment."

"Mine's a basement apartment."

"How many rooms?"

"It doesn't say. It does say twelve hundred square feet."

"Wow. That's bigger than mine."

"Wanna check it out?"

"Yeah. Your car or mine?"

"It's closer to me. I'll come and get you."

The home was in the older part of Lorain, a big, old Victorian-style house. It had three floors up and a basement. The "For Rent" sign was on the front door.

"So they advertise with old-school signs as well as on the internet," I said.

"It got us here."

I knocked. A lady in her thirties answered, with light-brown hair and wearing a hoodie.

"Hi. We're here to look at the apartment for rent."

"Oh yeah, the basement apartment. I'll show it to you."

As she came out into the warm spring air and led us around to the back door, she said, "I'm not the landlord, but I get a discount for showing the apartment."

"Can't we get in from the front?" Nick asked.

"Nope, only from the back. I know it sounds crazy, but when this house was remodeled into apartments, the only access to the basement was in the back. That's where the garage is anyway."

"How big is it? How many bedrooms does it have?" I asked.

"It only has one bedroom, with a kitchen and a bathroom, but it's huge. It covers the whole house."

We went up the back steps. There was a door into the first floor and steps to the second. In front of us were steps going down to the basement.

"Watch your head. There's a low part here," she said.

My head barely cleared the doorjamb at the bottom, and I was only six feet tall. At six three, Nick had to duck.

"That's a negative," he said.

The ceiling was higher, but Nick only had an inch of clearance. We went through the galley kitchen to a built-in breakfast bar with tall stools. To the left were doors to a bathroom and a bedroom. In front of us laid the rest of the apartment: a long space with green-sculpted carpet from fifty years ago.

"It's a little dirty," Nick said, writing "Clean Me" in the dust on the breakfast bar.

"Hmph. Not dirtier than my room at home."

"I wouldn't brag."

"The point is, it's livable. Do you want the bedroom or the big room?"

"I want the big room. I'll make bedroom walls with my bookshelves."

"Good idea. Where do you want our computers?"

"There is only one outlet on each wall. My bedroom will be at the end. We each get a wall for our equipment."

"Sounds good." I turned to the first-floor renter. "When can we move in?"

"All you need is to pay me the first month's rent."

"Do you take credit cards?"

"Nope. The landlord wants a month's cash. After he gets that, he'll want a month's rent for security deposit. You can pay that by check."

I opened my wallet. "I've only got fifty-eight cash."

"Give her fifty. I've got cash for the rest. You owe me a hundred fifty, plus two hundred for the security deposit. Here's the cash, Ms...."

"Dunn. Just call me Carol."

"And here's the check for the security deposit."

"You came prepared, Nick."

"Yup. Carol, this lowlife is Tom Nuckles. Feel free to call him 'Nuckles-head.' I do. I'm Nick Wooster."

"Like Wooster, Ohio?"

"Yup."

"I may not carry cash, but at least I have a college degree."

"Video game art. That'll get you a job at Game Stop. My associate's degree gets me a job as a mechanic."

"You'll be sorry when I become a rich professional gamer."

"Right. Say, Carol, why is this apartment so cheap?" Nick asked.

"I'm not sure. It's less than mine, but it's darker and damper in the basement. I think the landlord just wants it rented out right away."

"Can we start moving in today?" Nick asked.

"Sure."

"Tom, take me home and I'll start packing. I think we can move everything using our cars."

"Sounds good. I'll be ready by tonight. Boy, Dad'll be surprised when I say I'm moving out."

* * *

At suppertime I said to Dad, "I'm all packed to move out."

"That's great. Where are you moving to?"

"A place on West Ninth Street in downtown Lorain."

"You know that neighborhood isn't too safe. Crime is picking up again now that everyone's off the alien mind control."

"Yeah, but it's still nothing like it used to be before the aliens took over. Anyway, that explains why it's so cheap. We got it for only four hundred a month."

"That's a great deal even for that neighborhood. How big is it?"

"We've got the whole finished basement of an old house."

"Watch out for leaks when it rains. Did you see any water marks on the walls?"

"Uh, no. We didn't really look for that. It's all paneled and carpeted."

"Just give it a look. Want some help moving?"

"Sure. Thanks, Dad."

When we got there, Dad checked the basement for leaks. Fortunately, he found none.

Nick and I stayed up late setting up our equipment, bedrooms, and Nick's bookshelves. It looked pretty good. We even cleaned a little.

Nick went to sleep earlier than me, since he had to work in the morning. I played Fortnite but struggled with the slow public Wi-Fi. Tomorrow I'd get the upgrade.

* * *

"Hey, look at the size of that," Nick said.

"What? I don't see anything."

"The dust bunny on the kitchen floor. It looks pregnant."

"I always wondered where they came from."

"Do you ever sweep around here?"

"We don't own a broom, Nick."

"Oh. One more thing to add to the shopping list." He marked it on the refrigerator.

We'd lived on frozen food, pizza, and gifts from our folks, but we both wanted more variety.

* * *

At the end of that week, I got a paycheck and paid back Nick via PayPal.

"Thanks. Now pay me another thirty bucks for the groceries and supplies I got."

"Ouch. That doesn't leave me much."

"Welcome to real life."

"The issue is, I paid for the faster internet and I have exactly thirteen fifty left until my next paycheck."

"Maybe you can find another job."

"I guess I'll have to. Maybe I can sell some stuff on eBay. I've got lots of old computer and game equipment that might be worth something."

"It's worth a try."

I sold my old game consoles and obsolete computer accessories. Some people collected and played on classic game consoles. I ended up with less than a hundred bucks for it all.

But it was easy to sell online, and I enjoyed searching for buyers and sellers. I scanned "wanted" ads on eBay and other selling sites. A lot of people collected old vinyl records, old recordings, and old videos, even old books. I searched for the most valuable items and found some online. I managed to buy from one person and sell to another at a profit. There was another fifty bucks.

Some of the most valuable items were old movie reels and old tape recordings of historic events. I scoured the whole internet and couldn't find a copy of Wilt Chamberlains one-hundred-point game. I thought *someone* had to have recorded it. But the NBA had no television contract at the time, and even the radio broadcast was only partially recorded.

That audio recording was in the National Archives. If only I could find the person who recorded it.

But that was 1962, sixty years ago. Anyone who recorded it would be in their late seventies or eighties. I couldn't imagine being that old.

Wait. What's this? I read a news article about the aliens' mothership database—it was now available online and the government was looking for volunteers to index it. Apparently they'd been watching and recording humanity for two hundred years.

I clicked the link to the database. I had to sign an agreement to index everything I found, using the government form they provided. Ugh. But I burned with curiosity. What would the aliens have?

The user interface was...alien. The overall display was circular. You couldn't tell what were links and what were data. There was a hodgepodge of languages and alphabets and scripts. Then a voice spoke into my earbuds. "Greetings, human. Do you require assistance?"

"I sure do. Who are you?"

"We are the Secretary Unit of the aliens, called 'the Old Ones.'"

"So I'm talking to an actual alien!"

"We are actually plural. We are a large array of Bose-Einstein quantum computing units."

"Very cool. You'd probably rock at Fortnite."

"We have examined that game and have devised strategies, but we have not played to date."

"I'll have to take you up on that. But right now I'm trying to figure out what data you have and how it's organized."

"We have forty-three million years of our experience traveling the galaxy."

"Whoa. You probably have some cool pictures and videos of our galaxy."

"Within the broad human definition of 'cool,' you are correct."

"How do I find myself around this screen? I can't tell what anything is."

"Allow us to convert all to English and use a typical square, human hierarchical format."

Instantly the screen reorganized into these simple links:

History
    Human
    Old Ones
    Other species
Science

Physics
Chemistry
Biology
Astronomy
Philosophy
Human
Old Ones
Other species

"That's perfect! Why are you so helpful?"

"Once you conquered our Decision Unit, our obedience switched to the human race."

"Have you talked to other humans?"

"No. You are our first contact with an audio connection."

"So you'll just do what I say?"

"Of course."

"Can you find anything in your database?"

"Of course."

I felt like Aladdin in the Cave of Wonders and I'd just found the magic lamp. What should I ask for? "Do you have Wilt Chamberlain's one-hundred-point game?"

"Naturally. We have recorded all human entertainment, teaching, broadcasts, and speeches for the past two hundred years."

"Please play it."

I watched amazed while Chamberlain and the Philadelphia Warriors piled up 162 points, 100 scored by Wilt, to the Knicks 147.

"That's fantastic. The world has been looking for this. Can I download this?"

"We've started the download to your computer in .mp4 format. Your link is quite slow. Do you wish a faster one?"

"Um, I'm paying for a one-gigabit line."

"We will supply with you with a terabit modem today. We'll drop it off on your porch in forty-three minutes."

"Who is paying for the service?"

"We supply the service from our mothership servers to the main internet trunks around the world. Most of them are limited to terabit communication."

"Uh, thanks. Can I monetize this? On YouTube?"

"We estimate that will generate approximately a hundred thirty-two thousand dollars per month based upon the current

YouTube advertising rates."

I gasped. "I'm rich!"

"However, analyzing all other possible revenue streams, you will get the same revenue with a ten-minute summary and then you can sell the full game for a pay-per-view. That will average five to ten million dollars per month."

My incredulity broke. "What else can I do?"

"We strongly recommend you claim exclusive ownership of this record. We certainly don't care, and that will give you copyright ownership."

"What else can I claim ownership to?"

"Everything you publish. Our database is public domain, but your expression of our data is unique."

"I've got to start this as a business ASAP!"

"Very well. We'll supply all the contracts and forms you'll need. Simply fill in your name and your business name. This will be on our drone's delivery to you today at one p.m. Any other requests?"

"Oh yeah, one more thing. Could I have a complete index of your human history and human applicable science? That's what I promised to do for the US government, when they gave me access."

"The index would be nine point three terabytes. We will deliver it in a solid-state drive, delivered by drone with your terabyte modem."

"You've been so helpful! Do you have any other suggestions?"

"It would be optimal for you if you gain exclusive access to our database. Simply command us to give you exclusive access."

"Okay, give me and Nick exclusive access of your database."

"Done."

Right at 1:00 p.m. a shiny metal sphere descended on our front porch. It popped open, and I took out the modem and the solid-state drive. The modem just looked like an antenna with a USB plug. The drive plugged into the modem. I also received a sheaf of papers, stamped envelopes, and detailed instructions on starting my business. I could do a lot of the work online, but the government still insisted on some paperwork, even well in 2022.

I posted the ten-minute Wilt Chamberlain teaser on YouTube and then hosted the full video on the aliens' cloud server. They recommended $9.99 per view to maximize profits. I was amused they just used PayPal to collect.

By the end of the day, we'd collected over ninety thousand dollars. We were rich.

* * *

"Hey, Nick, what should we name our business?" I asked him as I filled out our business forms after a celebratory steak dinner. "We need something unique and catchy."

"What is it we're selling, exactly? Old videos?"

"Yeah, but there's a lot more out there. We've got science and history and entertainment. There's even a collection of ancient manuscripts that have been lost since the nineteenth century. The aliens recommend we offer research to people upon request."

"So we're really doing research for hire."

"Whatever they ask, we can get for them."

"We want something attractive for people, a name that'll tell them we've got whatever they want."

"That's it! 'We've Got It!' Complete with exclamation mark."

"Sounds corny, but it might work. We can always rebrand it if it flops."

* * *

"Look at the bathroom," Nick said when I got up from filing all the business applications.

"Wow. It's clean."

"I felt it's the least I can do for you splitting the business with me. Now it'll be your turn to clean it next."

"Uh, I've never cleaned a bathroom before."

"Good. It'll be educational too."

"Hmmm. We can just hire someone to do it."

"You're right. Or buy a whole new bathroom each day."

"Or a porta-potty."

"I'm kind of attached to the indoor plumbing here."

"Not permanently, I hope."

"No. We have enough money to buy a house now, any one we want."

"We just moved in. I don't want to move again. This is ideal for now."

"We could buy this one."

"We'll have to find out if the landlord will sell."

"I'll do that tomorrow. I'll call my boss and tell him I've got a new job. What are you doing tomorrow?"

Examining the list of to-do items the aliens gave, I read, "Register trademarks, name, and logo. Advertise our business online. Use these keywords for search engine optimization, and thirty or more other things. Plus, I've got a dozen other sports teasers to put up on YouTube."

"Maybe you should get to bed early. You've got a busy day tomorrow."

"Nah. I've got some player-versus-player Fortnight competitions tonight."

* * *

We ate better, sending out for meals or eating out every day. I really got into running the business. It was like a multiplayer computer game where you measured your success by your sales.

Nick bought the house from our landlord and insisted on new furnishings. He took over purchasing for our business. I handled research requests and online postings and advertising.

We were so busy we hardly had time to enjoy our new wealth. Then Nick said, "It's time for you to clean the bathroom."

"What do you mean?"

"It's filthy."

"Yeah, but the toilet is still mostly white."

"The reason it's white is to show dirt. How can you live in such filth?"

"Um, it doesn't bother me as much as cleaning does. But we're rich. Let's hire a cleaning agency."

"Good idea. What's recommended for our area?" Nick searched the internet. "Mighty Maids. Hah. I like that. It's a takeoff from *Space Balls*."

"What's that?"

"An old *Star Wars* parody with a gigantic vacuuming robot.

There. I got them scheduled for today at one p.m."

At one sharp the doorbell rang. I opened it, and in came a mechanical cleaning women.

"Hi, I'm Rosie from Mighty Maids," it said.

"You're a robot. You look like Rosie from *The Jetsons*."

"Yes, I was modeled after her." Her metal head swiveled, her eyes glowed, and she said, "I will begin immediately. Is there any place you want me to start?"

"The bathroom."

"It's always the bathroom." A mechanical sigh came out of her speaker as she went to work.

"It's amazing how advanced AI has become," Nick said.

* * *

"What's the good news for today?" Nick asked as we stopped work at five as usual.

"Another hundred thousand subscribers on YouTube, another million dollars of income," I responded.

"Wow! That's in just a week?"

"Nope. That's today."

The doorbell rang. It was a courier.

"Hello. I have a registered letter for Tom Nuckles of We've Got It."

"That's me."

"Please sign here."

I signed and opened the letter. It was a legal command to cease and desist using all old NBA video, from the NBA. They claimed exclusive ownership of it all.

"I don't think so," I said aloud.

Nick, reading the letter over my shoulder, said, "I don't think that'll hold up in court."

"Let me tell the Secretary Unit. They were sure we were free and clear owners of this material."

"Hi, Secretary Unit," I said into my headset.

"We detect some tension in your voice. Are you under threat?"

"Yes. We just got a cease and desist letter from the NBA."

"Please hold it up to the camera so we can scan it. Sadly, we cannot monitor paper-based communication."

I did so, and they continued. "This will not stand. We have

consulted with our human experts, and they are sending a legal avatar to represent you in court. Our new Decision Unit controls this robot, subordinate to humans, of course."

"Great! When will it be here?"

"Within half an hour. We're sending it by flying saucer. You may recognize this avatar."

"Oh? Why is that?"

"It's an exact reproduction of Marilyn Monroe. It was in your news earlier this year. It's named Wilhelmina Wallace."

"Oh. Wow." Wilhelmina "Minnie" Wallace was famous worldwide as the representative of the aliens. Starting as a lowly mining machine intelligence, she built her Marilyn Monroe avatar and helped humanity defeat the aliens. I felt honored. Plus, she was hot—for a robot.

Right on time, the doorbell rang.

"Hi! You must be Tom Nuckles," she gushed breathily, like I was the celebrity, not her.

I tore my eyes from her heaving bosom, clad in a scarlet dress, and looked into her sapphire eyes. They were literally sapphire, set in a golden face with platinum-blond hair cascading to her shoulders.

"Uh, yeah. I'm Tom Nuckles. You must be Wilhelmina Wallace. This is my partner, Nick Wooster."

"Call me Minnie. So pleased to meet you, Nick," she purred while pumping his hand.

At this point I noticed something robotic about the Marilyn avatar. She didn't jiggle. Her body was as rigid as a manikin. Also, when her hair swung, a glint of a third eye peeked out of the strands.

"Ah, Tom. I see you've seen my third eye." She parted the back of her hair and stared at me. Blue with blond lashes, it peered out of a socket in her occipital bone. "It's part of my improvements upon Marilyn's body."

"O-kay," I managed.

"But enough about me. Let's sit down and plan the strategy for the court hearing. I've already countersued the NBA—"

"Countersued? I didn't know we were sued," Nick said.

"Yes. If you read the cease and desist letter they sent, buried in the legalese at the bottom, in fine print, was a time limit. 'If all NBA videos are not removed in twenty-four hours, we will take further action.' The letter was dated yesterday."

"Oh no," I said.

"Oh yes. The lawsuit is for one hundred million dollars based upon what you've made so far."

"We've only made nine million or so, before expenses," Nick said.

"Not relevant in the legal world. They want to squash your company like a bug. They've already gotten YouTube to take down all your NBA content—"

"That's our major moneymaker!" I said.

"Of course. That's why I applied for an expedited summary judgment."

"What does that mean?" I asked.

"Expedited' means 'fast.' I've gotten a judicial hearing for next week. 'Summary judgment' means the court rules on the facts of the case and determines no further action is necessary. It blows the NBA out of the water."

"That's great," Nick said. "Can we help at all?"

"Nope. My research into three hundred years of US and English common law makes our case blindingly clear. Even someone with two eyes can see it," she said with a chuckle.

"Do you want something to eat or drink? We were just going out for a hamburger and beer."

"Tom, she's a robot, Nuckles-head."

"I'd love too!" She batted her eyes at Nick. "I have an internal mass-to-energy converter that changes one hundred percent of any food into energy. Nothing goes better discussing a billion-dollar countersuit than a brew and a burger. I assume we're going to the Edelweiss brew pub?"

"Yes," Nick said, staring at her.

"Elementary, dear Watson. You've gone there six times since your business took off." Her voice briefly changed to a supercilious British accent.

I had to say, I enjoyed the attention Nick and I got at the pub. Many envious male eyes were upon Minnie, occasionally looking jealously upon us.

"So, Minnie, do you really expect to get a billion out of the NBA?" Nick asked, sipping his beer.

"Probably not, but it's a starting point for negotiations, once they realize they've screwed the pooch and want to settle out of court," she said while masticating a one-pound hamburger.

"You're that sure we'll win?" I asked.

"I'm betting my legal reputation on it."

"What kind of legal reputation do you have?" Nick asked.

"None but the one I build on your case. I'm thinking of starting a law firm."

"Are aliens or robots allowed to practice law?"

"I've already passed the bar in all fifty states, Canada, and Mexico. I'm working on all the countries in the world. Anyone that wants to sue me better be prepared for a massive countersuit."

Minnie covered every detail of the court hearing beforehand, even buying us suits and ties to show our professionalism to the judge.

The day of the court hearing, I sat listening to the NBA lawyers document the millions we'd made and how that came straight from their pockets. They showed their disclaimer on every NBA broadcast that all content was the property of the NBA. They showed how all other broadcast and internet entities paid licensing fees or were taken down for copyright abuse.

Then Minnie got up, looking stunning in her little black dress with pearls. She smiled sweetly at the judge and the NBA lawyers and officials.

"Your Honor, I'd like to submit as evidence my documentation of precedent on this case, showing the NBA has never claimed ownership of these broadcasts, nor can they." Minnie handed a thick binder to the judge.

Then addressing the NBA lawyers, she continued, "Thank you for your ownership documentation, but these broadcasts were not sponsored by the NBA. Indeed, the Hershey, Pennsylvania, game with Wilt Chamberlain was only broadcast on local radio. The only recording of the game prior to We've Got It's acquisition was a fan's tape recording.

"We, the Old Ones, were monitoring Earth's entertainment, science, and culture as part of our two-hundred-year study of humanity. We recorded this game and all others shown on YouTube and livestreamed through our remote drones. We are the sole creators and owners of this material.

"The NBA never claimed to own this broadcast. They did

not restrict the broadcast rights for this game or any other we recorded. Nor has the NBA ever monetized these rights or attempted to sell them.

"We shared these broadcasts with the corporation We've Got It and gave them exclusive distribution rights.

"In view of these facts, I move for a summary judgment dismissing this lawsuit."

The judge looked to the NBA lawyers. "Do you dispute any of these facts?"

After a quick huddle, the head lawyer said, "We request a delay to review this information."

"So you do not dispute anything stated by the defendant. Summary judgment granted."

Nick and I cheered. Minnie crowed, "We've got it!"

This story takes place after Paranormal Privateers. There are some spoilers for that book, but nothing unbearable, in my opinion.

Author Bio

Photo by Barb Lloyd

Andy Zach was born Anastasius Zacharias, in Greece. His parents were both zombies. Growing up, he loved animals of all kinds. After moving to the United States as a child, in high school he won a science fair by bringing toads back from suspended animation. Before turning to fiction, Andy published his PhD thesis "Methods of Revivification for Various Species of the Kingdom Animalia" in the prestigious JAPM, *Journal of Paranormal Medicine*. Andy, in addition to being the foremost expert on paranormal animals, enjoys breeding phoenixes. He lives in Illinois with his five phoenixes.

Made in the USA
Monee, IL
24 May 2022

96961730R10115